WANT YOU

FINDING LOVE SERIES - BOOK 1

JOANNE DANNON

CLARENDON 3
PUBLISHING

CONTENTS

COPYRIGHT

ISBN:(Kindle) 978-1-925450-52-1

ISBN: (epub) 978-1-925450-53-8

ISBN: (print) 978-1-925450-54-5

ISBN: (large print) 978-1-925450-47-7

Dewey Number: A823.4

Want You - edited in UK English

This is a work of fiction. Names, characters, businesses, places, events, and incidents are either the products of the author's

WANT YOU

JOANNE DANNON

*H*ollywood megastar Sam Balfer returns to Australia to promote his new block-buster hit. But encountering Paige Dalton, a blast from his past, changes everything.

WHEN PAIGE ENDS up on Sam's arm for a red-carpet event, it's a walk that she never imagined. She's hidden her feelings for him since the days she tutored him in math and science. They were just friends—despite how much she wished their chemistry was off the charts.

BUT PAIGE IS JUST the quirky little nerd, the ugly duckling next to her younger and more glamorous sisters. However, Sam is suddenly beginning to see her as so much more.

AND SO IS the entire world—now that the tabloids blasted their kiss all over everything. Paige and Sam must confront their true feelings for one another with every set of eyes on them.

BUT WITH AN OCEAN separating them and the press broadcasting their every move, Paige is in over her head. She may have gotten the guy, but her guy is a star. Can this ordinary girl deal with this actor's superstar life?

Joanne Dannon has been living in the world of romance for as long as she can remember. From doodling hearts on her school notebooks to regularly reading romances, Joanne's world has always been filled with the excitement of love stories. So it was just a natural for Joanne to begin writing the genre she's always loved.

Formerly a policy writer by day and romance writer by night, Joanne now works full time writing the books she adores. Creating heroes for readers to fall in love with and heroines to cheer on, her characters are people readers can identify with.

Joanne writes to give her readers the experience she still loves to savour—indulging in a sigh-worthy happily-ever-after, being swept away from the everyday by diving into a delicious romance novel.

Joanne Dannon is a happily married mother of two heroes-in-training who loves spending time with friends and family. She can be found on Facebook and her website www.joannedannon.com chatting about reading, writing, cooking, vintage-inspired dresses and all things romantic. She loves to hear from readers.

Sign up to her newsletter and to say thanks, Joanne will send you a free copy of Bidding on Love. Go to www.joannedannon.com

www.joannedannon.com
joanne@joannedannon.com

DEDICATION

For my friends who also have a crush on actor, Sam Heughan

"Tell me you're joking," Paige Dalton shouted at her best friend. "Tell me you didn't waste money that you should be saving for *your* wedding on me."

Paige and Rachel were seated across from each other, in a hidden bar, down one of Melbourne city's laneways.

Rachel King, her best friend since high school, flicked her hair over her shoulder like she didn't have a care in the world. "It's my money," she sniffed.

Paige's eyes narrowed. "You're getting married next year, and you wasted your savings on me. Why?" What had possessed her friend to spend money on her, especially since her fiancé, Travis, was so uptight about their finances? But as they sat in the trendy wine bar, it seemed that Rachel had forgotten all about Travis, and her focus was on her bestie.

Rachel's lips twitched, like she was really enjoying the moment. "Who's your celebrity free pass?" Rachel cocked an arrogant eyebrow at her friend. "Hmmm?" She took a sip of her espresso martini.

Embarrassment coursed through her veins at the reminder of her pass. She'd had a massive crush on him for so many years, she couldn't remember a time she hadn't. Those dark eyes. Those sensual lips.

Her breath came rushing out. "You know it's Sam Balfer. The guy I secretly pined for in high school, the guy who is now Hollywood's hottest actor," Paige flung at her friend. In his teens, Sam had been cute, and she'd doodled her name and his in her chemistry book. Now he was hot and in demand by Hollywood's elite. He'd starred in so many movies, and had a league of women who wished they could be Mrs Balfer. . . including her. Not that she was going to share that with her friend. She tried to divert the conversation. "Everyone has a leave pass." She sniffed before glaring at her friend. "I can't believe we're having this conversation."

"None of my friends tell their potential

boyfriends, *upfront*, about it." Rachel's hands sat on her hips. "Seriously, Paige, who does that?" The dramatic roll of her eyes was softened by the twitch of Rachel's lips. She was enjoying this more than she should. Thank goodness it was only the two of them out tonight. She'd be mortified if another friend or sister heard Rachel speak.

Paige felt her face redden. She'd had only a handful of boyfriends, so it didn't seem weird to mention it upfront, and secondly, she never expected to ever see Sam again. Look at who he was. And then look at her. She shook her head. Sam dated glamorous models and actresses, and she. . .she dated anyone who was taller than her. Basically, her dates needed to be at least six foot. Yet another reason why she could count the number of boyfriends she'd had on one hand.

"Paige, Travis and I have been together for years, and we're going to get married. Guess what?" She paused for dramatic effect. "We don't have an agreement like that?"

Paige felt her forehead crease in surprise. "Really, I thought all couples did that." Didn't everyone have a celebrity they lusted after? Didn't couples have these understandings? She scratched her head, sure that was not unusual. Surely other couples accepted these *passes*?

Rachel pointed at her friend's blush and chuckled. "Only you would add a clause like that to the start of all your relationships." She paused. "So that's why I entered you in the competition...many times."

"How many times?" she whispered. She felt as if time slowed as she waited for her friend to fess up.

Rachel pretended to admire her manicured nails, knowing full well the effect the delay was having on her friend. "Um, I stopped counting at fifty," she said in a manner that showed she was unfazed at how much money she'd just blown on a competition.

Paige was sure her stomach fell and splattered on the floor. Rachel had to be joking. "What? You have to make a donation for every entry, it's not cheap."

"I wanted you to have a winning chance at Sam," she implored, as though spending money on Paige winning a contest was not foolhardy or silly.

"Let me get this right." She wagged her forefinger at her friend. "You've used some of your wedding money, and done fundraising so I have a chance at winning a date with Sam Balfer."

"Yep," Rachel said so the p at the end of yep came out as a popping noise. "We watched the video together and I saw you literally swoon during it. I swear you licked your lips so many times, and if your tongue was long enough it would've hit the floor."

Rachel grinned. "One lucky woman gets a dream date with Sam when he comes to Australia next month. Why shouldn't it be you? Your choice of location. Climbing Sydney Harbour Bridge at sunrise, snorkelling at the Great Barrier Reef, romantic dinner in the outback watching the sunset over Uluru, the list goes on." She paused. "How good would it be if you won?"

"You're nuts." She took a deep breath. "This video has gone viral, there are thousands of women who are entering the competition to win a date with Sam. I mean, who wouldn't want to?" She had no chance of winning a date with Sam. She didn't want to admit that she'd already entered twice in the hope she'd win.

But for now, she needed to berate her friend.

Rachel raised her hand and said with honesty, "Not me, he's not my type."

"What? Your type doesn't include swoon-worthy handsomeness with piercing dark eyes?"

"Just kidding, he is gorgeous," Rachel admitted with a wink. "Anyway, I can't win. You'd kill me. You're the one with the giant-sized crush on him that doesn't seem to have wavered over the past twelve years or so."

Thirteen years and four months to be precise, but

she wasn't going tell that to Rachel. Paige looked at the cushion in her hand and wondered whether to hit her friend with it, or smother her with it. "Travis will kill you when he learns what you did."

"What he doesn't know won't hurt him. It's not that much money. . . compared with a wedding," Rachel admitted. "A friend is making the cake and I found a dress online to save on costs."

"You're not getting that dress you found last week? The one you loved? The one you wanted with all your heart?" she uttered in disbelief that her friend was missing out because of *her*.

"It's a dress," she said with reassurance and a toss of her hair. "I will be wearing it once. Spending thousands of dollars is ridiculous. This online dress is pretty and very similar." It sounded so practical but Paige's heart ached. Rachel had loved that dress, said it was her dream dress, and she'd looked breathtakingly beautiful in it.

Rachel was giving up so much for *her* that a wave of sadness engulfed her. Rachel was like her sister, and part of her family. She loved Rachel as much as she loved her three sisters. Giving up a dress so she had a chance to win the dream of a lifetime... spending time with Sam.

It was very special that Rachel had done this, but

the chances of her winning were so slim. She massaged the skin above her breast, to ease the ache that lingered there.

RACHEL WAVED her hand in the air as though dismissing what her friend said. "So maybe now is not the time to tell you that I also wrote to Sam's publicist about you?" she asked in a chirpy voice, as though the bombshell was as simple as them ordering another round of drinks.

Paige clasped a hand over her mouth to stop the expletive from firing from her lips. She mentally replayed what her friend had just announced before she asked, "Tell me this is a nightmare, and I'm going to wake up?"

Rachel leaned over and pinched her friend's arm, hard.

"Ouch," she rubbed her arm. "What was that for?"

Rachel wiggled her eyebrows. "Proving this is not a nightmare or a dream. It's really happening. I did this for you, because I love you." She blew her a kiss. "Besides you've always wanted a chance with Sam, and now you have one. You're welcome." She took a long sip of her martini before leaning back in her chair, arms loosely crossed over her chest and a smug grin on her face.

Silver spots danced across Paige's eyes. Stunned didn't even come close to how she was feeling. If Sam's publicist knew about the stupid crush, then surely Sam would find out. Her stomach knitted in mortification, and her limbs grew heavy. "This is ridiculous. I'm almost thirty, I had a crush on him at school."

Rachel shrugged as though her friend's discomfort was not something to focus on. "Like I didn't know that." She paused. "I know you've always wondered what would've happened if you'd told him how you felt, back then that is. You know, when you were helping him study."

Paige laid a hand over her breastbone as wishful thinking took her back to those school years when she'd tutored him in science and maths. How many times had she wished he'd suddenly turn around and notice her, really notice her? Not just see her as the smart, nerdy girl. "Well you know me. I'm not Phoebe. She would've said something…not me. Not that she would've had that issue. Sam would've noticed her for sure." Paige smiled pensively. "I may have been blessed with a high IQ, but Phoebe got the brains and the beauty. No wonder she's a model, and I'm…an engineer."

"Maybe, but she hasn't eaten chocolate for years. Who wants to be a model when you can't eat?"

Paige's lips twitched with amusement. "That's true. She'd never have eaten the yummy dumplings we had tonight."

"You see," her friend pointed to her. "It's not always easy being Phoebe."

Paige shrugged pretending that her lack of looks didn't worry her. Sure, she was proud of her sister, but there were times that she wished she was a little prettier. She drained the remainder of her drink as she focussed on her thoughts.

Shaking her head, she said, "Rachel, Sam's video has gone viral. The chance of me winning is so remote. I'm sorry you've wasted your money."

Her friend leaned towards her. "But—"

"Rach, the thought was really nice, it's beautiful and heartfelt but you shouldn't have done it." She let out a dramatic breath. "And even if I won, just saying I did. What then? You think some gorgeous, highly paid actor who struts the red carpet and earns millions for each movie he does would be interested in me? Seriously?"

"Maybe not, but you'd have the time of your life. A night to remember." Rachel's eyes lit up as though imagining Paige and Sam at the Academy Awards together, arms around each other, giving each other secret smiles.

"And then what?" She felt her shoulders sag with

disappointment. The date would be over. All that excitement and planning...and then it would be over. She'd get one night with him, something so special that she could scarcely dream of it happening to her. It was what she wished for, with all her heart...that she would be chosen. Her heart sighed with contentment at the thought of being alone with him on a dream date.

"I'm sorry Paige, I really thought you'd love the idea." Rachel's sincere words interrupted thoughts of her and Sam snorkelling together in the balmy waters in Queensland. Her friend hopped off her seat and walked over, giving her a large bear hug.

Paige snuggled into the warmth of her friend's embrace. This was true friendship. This was what she could rely on, a best friend who'd never let her down. "I really do, but this is real life, not a fairy tale or romance movie." She took a deep breath. "We've known each other too long for me to think this was me winning a date with Sam. I want to know the real reason why you came up with this hairbrained idea."

Rachel bit her lip and her cheeks flushed red under the scrutiny of her glare. Bingo. She was right. She'd known Rachel too long for there not to be other motivation behind this Sam-date thing.

"Come on, spill it." She encouraged. "I'm sure it's

not as embarrassing as Sam's publicist knowing about my teen crush on her client."

Rachel rubbed her chin. She opened her mouth but nothing came out. After clearing her throat a couple of times, she said, "Um, since you're on a break with Mike, I thought that being with Sam would make you see that Mike is not the right guy for you."

"What?" She blinked rapidly as she digested what Rachel had just said. "Mike and I had been seeing each other for six months, and you're telling me now?" She shook her head as though eliminating her friend's comments from her memory.

Mike had been pressuring for her to move in with him. Rachel knew that but she'd never said anything till now.

She still wasn't sure if Mike was the guy for her, hence the break. She liked him but had wondered if she was settling for comfortable. Or perhaps that stupid crush on Sam was affecting the way she saw their relationship. She really needed to get over her teen crush. "Mike's a nice guy. He's not only taller than me, he doesn't mind that I skateboard, and he admires my work."

Rachel's shoulders slumped. "I don't know. You just don't seem right for each other. I think it was a good idea to have a break."

"He's been hinting at getting married. I don't know what to think. A break seemed like a good idea for me to work things out." Paige reached over and took her friend's hand in her own. "You are like a sister to me. I'm sorry you don't like him. If there is something specific you can tell me, I'll always listen to what you have to say."

"No, nothing," she said with honest dismay. "But when you see someone dating Sam, you remember that you had a chance with him and blew it."

Paige spluttered. "I have no chance with Sam. Winning a date with him is like winning the lottery."

"Whatever," she replied.

"Don't *whatever* me," she flung at her friend.

Rachel finished her martini and then waved to the bartender. "Two more please," she gave him a smile that had him giving her a thumbs-up.

"You see, you're gorgeous, and the guy is doing what you asked him. If I did that, he'd wave me over to take my order." Paige rolled her eyes.

"Phoebe is stunning, like seriously gorgeous but it's intimating being next to her," her friend confessed.

"Is that why you're friends with me and not her?" Paige sniggered, knowing full well that the bond between them was special, and also Phoebe was six years younger than her. That was a big age differ-ence when they were in high school.

"You're more down to earth, and besides, you helped me with maths and science at school. My own private tutor," she cooed, playing along.

"So basically, you like my intelligence, is that what you're saying?" Knowing full well that was not the reason they were besties. They'd spent more time talking about boys, cute rock stars and their favourite songs than doing maths.

Rachel cocked a finger gun at her and fired it. "Got it in one, babe."

The bartender brought over two espresso martinis and Rachel thanked him with a large smile. "Thanks."

"Call me," the cute guy said. "Number's on the receipt."

Rachel gave him a wink, but when the bartender's back was to them, she rolled her eyes. "No, thanks," she said to Paige.

"You have guys hitting on you all the time, are you sure you want to marry Travis?" Paige asked, dismissing the niggle of jealousy in her belly. When they were out together, guys were always falling over themselves to talk to her bestie. It was yet another reminder of how plain she was, and why Sam would never be interested in someone like her.

Rachel grinned. "Of course I do. Besides, I'm just flirting, and no, I'm not going to call him." Her head nodded towards the barman.

They clinked glasses. "To us," Paige toasted.

"To you meeting Sam next month, and to me having a fab life with Travis," Rachel said.

"Cheers," they said in unison.

a week later, early in the morning as Paige was dressing for work, her mobile phone rang. Curious to who'd call at seven in the morning, she answered it.

"Paige Dalton?" A woman's voice asked.

"Yes, I'm Paige." Her breath quickened, wondering why a woman with an American voice was calling her.

"Hi Paige, I'm Leonie Michaels, I'm Sam Balfer's publicist."

The air whooshed out of her lungs, her legs felt as stable as wet paper mâché, so she collapsed on the nearest chair. "How can I help you?" Her heart raced and her breathing became rapid.

"Your friend, Rachel King, has written to me a number of times about you winning the *Date with*

Sam contest." Leonie's clipped voice sounded out, seemingly unaware of the panic attack that was making Paige's hands shake.

"I'm so sorry about that, I had no idea." Her mouth and lips felt as dry as desert sand, and she licked them twice.

"We can't make you the winner, not only is that unethical, it's immoral." Leonie's voice came across as stern as a school principal.

"Of course." She was still cringing about the whole Sam-date-entry debacle that Rachel had created.

Leonie continued. "Sam is coming out to Australia in two weeks to promote his latest movie. It's a romantic comedy, and a first for him."

And?

"We're premiering the movie in his home town, Melbourne," Leonie paused. "And he needs a date. I think it would be a good idea if *you* were his date."

What? Paige felt dizzy, and if she wasn't already sitting down, she would've fallen down. Leonie wanted her to be Sam's date? She squeezed her eyes shut, counted to five and then asked, "Did you tell me that I will be Sam's date for the movie premiere?" Still unable to believe what Leonie had suggested.

"Yes, I'll email you the details. You need to meet him at his hotel, you'll be chauffeured to the movies with Sam and walk down the carpet with him. You need to dress up and be available Tuesday the seventh of next month. I'll also email you an NDA which includes expectations of your behaviour for the night," she said, not pausing for a breath. She probably had never encountered someone who'd say no to being with Sam.

"Umm. . ."

"You're deciding whether to be Sam's date for two hours?" Her voice was filled with surprise. "Rachel said you've had a crush on him since school, I thought you'd jump at the chance. It's a once-in-a-lifetime opportunity."

Paige's bones dissolved from the embarrassment and shame of some woman in America, who she didn't know, who worked for Sam knowing this. "You want me to walk down the red carpet with Sam, at the premiere of his movie?"

"Yes," she snapped making Paige feel that she was wasting this woman's time, and that she had better things to do than deal with some star-struck fan.

A million emotions and questions raced through her head. And the answers all started with no. How could she do it? Sam would know? She wasn't glam? Everyone would laugh at her.

"We're going with a friendship angle, which will suit Sam and the movie. Over the past few years, he's focussed on dramas and historical movies but *Home-coming* is a fun romance, and I think him having a childhood friend as a date will work well with his image." Leonie continued, which gave her some reassurance. Surely it wouldn't be too bad?

"Um, so Sam will think it's just a date with a friend?" she asked tentatively, feeling as silly as a teen. "He won't know about Rachel and her emails to you?" Her chest tightened, imaging Sam knowing about her friend's ploys to get them together.

Leonie let out a frustrated breath, and Paige was sure she was rolling her eyes. "I'm his PR rep, and my job is to do what's best for Sam, not you." She paused. "He won't question me on my decisions, I've been working with him for too long. And no, I won't tell him about your crush."

The air whooshed out of her lungs. "Okay, I'll do it."

"Of course you will. Who'd say no to a night out with Sam?" she said with an incredulous tone. "Is this your email address?" She read it out correctly.

"Yes, it is," she replied in a soft voice, unable to believe she'd just agreed to be Sam's date for a couple of hours.

She needed help. Help so that she didn't make an idiot of herself and look ridiculous. Her standard look was jeans, sneakers, and T-shirts. That look would not be suitable.

"You should thank your friend for contacting me, you're very lucky to get this opportunity," Leonie continued, seemingly unaware of the concerns she was battling. "Don't let me down. If you do, you'll be letting Sam down. Bye."

She disconnected the call and Paige sat there, her mouth open, staring at the phone, still unable to believe what had just happened. She. Was. Going. To. See. Sam.

Oh. Em. Gee.

She quickly rang in her friend, and the words tumbled out, matching the rhythmic pounding of her heart. "You emailed Sam's PR woman, right? She just rang me. I'm going on a date with Sam. Not the competition one, but to see a movie. And I don't know what to wear. I'm scared that I'll trip over and then Sam will look like an idiot for inviting someone as clumsy as me as his date."

There was silence. "Rach? Are you there?"

A high-pitched squeal rang out, and Paige had to move the phone from her ear. "I think you just woke up every dog in the neighbourhood."

"I can't believe it, you're going to see Sam. We have to make you look fab, then he'll kiss you and take you back to LA."

"What?" If her nerves were shot to pieces, her friend's words did little to calm the anxiety in her belly.

Rachel chuckled. "Sorry, just wishful thinking."

She nibbled on her fingernail. "Rach, what do I do about Mike?"

"Not only are you on a break but you have a celebrity pass *baby*. Woo hoo."

She cleared her throat. "It's unlikely that Sam'll want to do anything with me except catch up on friends we went to school with. And besides, I'm not his type."

Rachel squealed once more. "I can't believe you and Sam. On. A. Date. I'm a genius." She could almost see her friend congratulating herself with a pat on the back. "This is even better than I could've hoped for."

"Okay, yes, that was very clever of you to organise and I am thankful, even if I want to kill you at the same time." That was true. She was still deciding if she was going to kiss or kill her friend next time she saw her.

"That's what friends are for," she sang to her, the lyrics from the hit song, popular in the 1980s. "When's the premiere?" Rachel's voice was filled with excitement and anticipation.

"On the seventh." Paige sneaked a look at her

notes, yep, it was the seventh. Seven was her lucky number so she hoped that would be an auspicious day.

"That's only a week away, we have so much to do." She paused. "Please tell me Phoebe is in town."

"Phoebe is in town," she parroted back to her friend.

"Oh, thank goodness," Rachel breathed a big sigh of relief.

Paige gave her friend an exaggerated *pfft*. "Of course she's not. Silly. She's a model working for an international company, she lives in London." Paige flung at her friend. "Seriously. What are we going to do? I can't wear jeans and runners." Her right ankle bobbed, her leg bounced up and down as nerves made it hard for her to sit still.

"Um, let me think." She could hear her friend's fingers drumming on something...a table?

"I need a drink." Paige muttered an expletive under her breath. She couldn't balance the sheer excitement of seeing Sam again against not having a suitable ensemble to wear. After all, she did want to look fabulous, even for an engineer. She'd never look as glamourous as her model sister, and that was fine with her. But she did want to look good. She'd be seen with Sam at a public event, it wasn't some private affair. What would she wear?

"It's the morning, have a coffee instead," Rachel snapped at her. "This is such an opportunity, and all you care about is what to wear. Aren't you excited about seeing him again?"

"I will be once I know that I won't be turning up in jeans. And I'm also worried about tripping, you know how clumsy I am," she confessed in a low voice. Her knees were often bruised as she tripped over the edges of carpet, walked into closed doors or knocked into the sides of office cubicles. She tried to avoid them, she really did. But unlike her sisters, who seemed to be able to navigate through life without so much as a fall, she was the laughing stock of her family. If anyone was going to end up flat on her face, it would be her. Gah!

"You'll be fine, and even if you're not, I'm sure Sam will catch you in his strong, manly arms." Rachel chuckled at her own joke.

Paige swallowed hard. Knowing all too well the definition of his *strong, manly arms*.

Rachel snapped her fingers. "Your cousin Jasmine, what about her? She's super cool and she'll know what to wear."

"You're a genius Rach, she's perfect." Jasmine was a second cousin or something like that. They were almost the same age but Paige was often intimidated by how gorgeous Jas was. She effortlessly wore teeny-tiny dresses that displayed her toned body to perfection. If she didn't love Jas so much, she'd be jealous of her. "But um, let's not say who I'm meeting," she said, as worry niggled her. Would Jasmine believe that someone like her had a date with Sam?

"No way, she needs to know the importance of getting your outfit right," her friend fired back. "I can't believe you're going on a date with Sam Balfer, Mr Gorg-alicious. I bet he kisses like a dream."

Yep, she bet he did, too. Shame she wouldn't find out through first-hand knowledge. "I don't think we'll be kissing," she said with a disappointed sigh. "He's famous. We probably won't be on our own at all. He'll have his hangers-on, and then all his fans. . ." Her forehead rested in her palms as visions of her and Sam surrounded by screaming fans bombarded her brain. "What am I getting into?"

"The highlight of your life, babe," Rach said with a jubilant tone. "The best thing that is gonna happen to you. Except, being my Maid of Honour at my wedding."

SHE'D WORKED like a robot during the day, unable to focus on her work and the emails that needed replying to. After re-reading an important email a number of times, she realised that she was wasting her time. Plus, she didn't want to do anything that might jeopardise her career. She loved working at her job.

Leaving would be the smarter option, and she'd do some unpaid overtime to make up for the loss in her productivity. Pleading a headache, she was home by early afternoon but spent too much time pacing around her apartment as nervous energy pumped through her.

She desperately wanted to run along the beach to steady the stress she was feeling but was worried about a colleague seeing her. She hated lying to her manager, but she'd been as useless and uninspiring as a fruity cocktail at a guys' beer/footy night. She justified to herself that it was better that she came home and tried to focus on what she was going to say to Mike tonight. And she certainly didn't need to be a clairvoyant to know he would not be happy about her date with Sam.

Although Paige had suggested time apart when Mike suggested she move in, he hadn't understood what a "break" was and still treated her as his girl-friend. He still called her, dropped in and kept their relationship the same as it had been for the past few months. The only difference was that they hadn't had sex since she asked for time to think about *them*.

Paige felt it was the right thing to do, to discuss the date with Sam with Mike.

Later in the afternoon, unable to stay in her apartment, she walked the path along the beach, taking deep breaths to settle her rapidly beating heart. She tried meditation and positive thoughts but her mind was jumbled and she just couldn't focus on what she'd say to him.

Standing and looking out at the blue waters of Port Phillip didn't help her focus but she did feel calmer. An hour later, she returned home to make dinner. Mike would be over soon.

They sat at the small kitchen table opposite each other, and she tried to make a show of enjoying the chicken and vegetable stir fry dinner, one of the few things she could make without incinerating it.

Avoiding anything about herself, she kept her focus on Mike, his day at work, and any anecdotes he had to share. He didn't have many. He worked for a large supermarket chain and was the assistant manager at the store. Most of the time he talked about the complaints he dealt with from staff and customers. Rarely did he have any amusing stories that she would expect from a supermarket manager.

"You're not eating?" Mike pointed to her half-eaten meal.

"Um, I had cake this afternoon, it was someone's birthday." The lie rolled off her tongue.

"Whose birthday?" he asked, finishing his meal. "Mind if I finish yours?" Without waiting for her affirmative reply, he replaced his bowl with hers, and started eating the stir fry she hadn't been able to stomach.

She would've scolded him at his audacity, since it could've been her lunch for work the following day, but she was trying to work out whose birthday it was. Especially since there hadn't been a birthday or a cake. "Um, Janet's."

"You've never mentioned her," he said casually between mouthfuls of what should've been her lunch for tomorrow.

"She's um, a temp helping out." Lies, more lies. Her stomach clenched in response to her deception. It was so wrong.

Soon enough, she'd cleaned up while he checked his emails on his phone. After switching on the kettle, he stood and came over to nuzzle her neck. "I'm missing you, have you had enough time to think?"

There were times she wished he'd help her with the dishes or make her a tea. But no, he always had a reason why he couldn't help. *An urgent matter that had to be attended to*, was the most common excuse.

"You're all tense, baby," he said. "Let me massage that tension away." He massaged her shoulders and his breath warmed her skin before he pressed kisses along her shoulder.

"Um, I need to tell you something?" she started to say, pulling away from him.

She needed to tell him.

She was being a coward. She needed to be upfront and tell the man who wanted to marry her about Sam. It was a date, after all, nothing more.

"I need to talk to you about something that happened today," she said in a quiet voice. The nervous thump of her heart rang in her ears.

"Did you lose your job?" His eyes narrowed as he looked at her with annoyance.

"No, I didn't. Work is fine. Something funny happened to me today," she started to say as her muscles twitched with worry.

"You interrupted *me* to tell me a funny story. You couldn't have told me at dinner?"

She cleared her throat a couple of times. She sat opposite him, her hands clasped in her lap, her shoulders stiff and a forced smile on her lips. "Um, I got a phone call this morning. And um, I-ah, I um—"

"Can you tell me what's going on, you're making me nervous with all your ums." His lips pressed together, his eyes narrowed, his gaze focussed on her.

"Sorry. I've been invited to be Sam Balfer's date next week at the movie premiere of his new movie." The words tumbled out. She avoided anything about Rachel or Leonie. She just said it as it was.

A dark look crossed Mike's eyes. "I thought *we'd* decided that you weren't going to enter that *ridiculous* competition." He spat out the word ridiculous. "Seriously, you don't waste money to try and win a date with a celebrity. Especially Sam Balfer. Let some other loser go."

Her shoulders bristled with resentment. "I didn't win the competition. But, um, as Sam's new movie is a rom-com, they want his date to be a friend, someone he knows. I'll be attending the movie premiere with him. It's next week." She injected some enthusiasm into her voice.

"No." His eyes blazed with annoyance and his nostrils flared.

"What? What do you mean, no?"

"You heard me, I said no." His eyes seemed to bulge from their sockets, making her feel anxious and worried.

"You can't tell me what to do." Her jaw clenched with annoyance.

"I can and I just have." He crossed his arms over

his chest, giving off a vibe that the conversation was finished. . .well for him, it was.

She wanted to yell and punch him for the audacity of him telling her what to do. There'd been no compromise or understanding. "This is a big deal for me. I get to walk the red carpet with a friend and see a new movie. There's no harm in that. You know that I went to school with Sam."

"You want to have sex with him, so no," he said with a dismissive wave.

"Um, no. This is just two friends getting together. It's been organised by his publicist." Why did he have to demean her in such a way?

She looked at him and was surprised at the stiffness in his jaw and neck. His reddened face made her wonder if he was about to have a heart attack. "You're not going, and that's that."

She looked at him, her jaw opening but no words coming out. Finally, after what could've been seconds, minutes or hours, she said, "He's my celebrity pass."

He threw back his head and laughed. But it wasn't jovial, and his face grew more serious, if that was even possible. "You think you can use that?" He fired a look of animosity at her. "No. I'm not having some big-shot actor sticking his dick in you so he can add another notch to his bed head. There are enough others he can bed."

"Eww, really?" The image and his words were distasteful, and she was surprised at the venom in his tone. "It's a date, not some. . .groupie sex thing." She tried to justify her going.

"My fiancée doesn't sleep with anyone except me." He pressed his lips together, trying to end the discussion with his facial features.

She shook her head with annoyance. "We're not engaged, and we're on a break." Waving her pointy finger at him, she fired. "And you can't tell me what to do."

"I just did." His chin stuck out as the muscles in his forearms clenched.

She had the uncharacteristic urge to slap him across the face which she didn't, of course. She glared at him, her lips pressing tightly against one another. "We're not engaged."

He scrubbed a hand across his face. "You know it's what I want." His tone was softer, and she could see the regret in his eyes. "How can I be with you, knowing you've slept with someone else." He paused. "I'd never do that to you."

"It's a date, we'll be surrounded by heaps of other people." She tried desperately to reassure him. "We walk the red carpet, wave to fans, see the movie, and that's it."

"Really?" He shook his head. "You don't think the guy you've been fantasising about isn't going to want more? He's not only a man, but a star. He's used to getting what he wants, when he wants it."

"He doesn't know." She defended herself. "He won't know."

"Don't be stupid. He's a man, he'll see the desire in your eyes." He pinched the bridge on his nose as though he couldn't believe how ridiculous she was sounding.

"It won't be like that," she started to say, her hand waving his concerns away.

He came forward and gripped her shoulders, looking directly at her. "It will be like that. Trust me. I don't want you going near him." He released his hold on her, and returned his arms across his chest. "I agreed to your ridiculous..." he waved his had in the air. "Celebrity pass because I thought there was no chance you'd ever meet him."

Same with her. She never expected to pull the pass out. "It's just a—"

"No. You can't see him or meet up with him. He'll use you, that's what men like him do."

"Sam's not like that," she started to say.

"The last time you saw him was when you were

in high school. He's been in Hollywood for over ten years. You don't think he's changed. Of course he has. He's a star. He's got people fawning over him." He paused. "This is a guy that no one says no to."

"I'm almost thirty—" She'd changed since school, and so had Sam. She knew that.

"Baby, I love you, and you know that I want you in my life. But," he paused for dramatic effect. "You're not going. I can't bear the idea of you being with another man."

She stared at Mike, surprised at how passionate he was in his defence of her. He certainly hadn't been so vocal when she asked for some time to think about their future.

The date with Sam was harmless. There wouldn't be kissing, and there certainly wouldn't be sex. Sam would never be interested in her, not when he was surrounded by beautiful women in the industry.

But then she thought about her life ahead. Would she regret her decision? Would she ever have such a chance again? No, she wouldn't. Sam would return to Hollywood where he belonged.

Whereas she belonged in Melbourne with her parents, her sisters and her job. She and Sam were polar opposites. Unlike him, she'd never had any desire to seek out fame.

It would be one night.

One night that might break her.

Mike had been a considerate boyfriend but she wasn't sure if he was the one. If he was, wouldn't she have been happy to move in with him?

The break between them was supposed to help her decide. . .but it hadn't.

If she went on the date, but decided to go back to Mike, it would cause issues.

Was a date with Sam worth it?

What could Sam offer her? Nothing. She would be arm-candy, something there to enhance his image, not hers.

But this was the guy she'd had a massive crush on. . . for years.

Would she regret missing out on this opportunity?

The sensible option was to consider going back to Mike and cancel Sam. But an urge of such longing gripped her. She'd been sensible all her life.

The choice was not clear and she had no idea what to do.

CHAPTER 3

*P*aige slept fitfully and woke early that morning, her head filled with questions that all revolved around Sam.

Could she do it? Give up Mike for a date with Sam? Logically, it was the stupidest idea ever. She'd been with Mike for six months, so surely she should know if she was in love with him or not.

Apparently, she didn't. Because she wasn't sure what decision to make.

She needed good advice and a sister to chat with. Fortunately, she had three. She chose Paisley because despite being six years her junior, she was the most sensible of the three *options*.

It was early morning but she knew Paisley would be awake. She was a nurse, and a single mum, and

Paisley didn't look after herself as much as she looked after her young son.

Paisley answered the phone almost immediately. "Paige, what are you doing ringing me at this hour? Shouldn't you be asleep?"

"Good morning to you," she chuckled. "I wish. I have a dilemma and need advice."

"Good timing, Lev and I are in bed having early morning cuddles before he has his bottle of milk." Paisley paused. "Yes, it's your aunty Paige on the phone, yes, you have your milky while I talk," she cooed to Lev.

Paige smothered a smile at the baby talk. "Perhaps, I should call back?"

"No, I'm back from night shift and need sleep. But I need to be with him more. So while he drinks, I can chat."

"I'll come over on the weekend and look after him so you can have a sleep, if you like?" Paige suggested, loving the idea of spending time with her nephew. She loved this toddler stage, but couldn't wait till he was a little older so she could teach him to kick a footy and play sports.

She loved him as if he was her own. He was the sweetest boy, and as much as she hated Paisley being a single mum, there were times when she was secretly happy because it meant she had quality time with him. She adored spending time with her baby nephew.

Only the three sisters and their parents knew the secret identity of Lev's father. Paige hoped her sister could reconcile with him, let him know he had a gorgeous son. How many times had Paige wished to go behind her sister's back and tell him? But she hadn't. It wasn't for her to do. One day, she hoped Paisley would meet up with Lev's dad. She was managing fine as a single mum, but Lev needed a dad. Perhaps one day? She hoped so.

She blew out a long breath. "Okay, you need to help me," Paige said. "Thanks to Rachel, I won a date with Sam, as in Sam Balfer."

Paisley squealed. "Sam? Sam Balfer, the guy from school, who you had a secret crush on?" Paisley's voice was bursting with excitement. "You have a date with him?" She paused. "Did you hear that Levvie, your aunty Paige has a date with a Hollywood hottie."

"I do," she confessed to her sister, still unable to believe it had been organised.

"Why don't you sound excited. I'd expect you to have been jumping for joy, I mean, he's hot, and he was your friend all those years ago." There was concern in her sister's voice.

She cleared her throat. "I told Mike last night and

he's gone all possessive over me, and doesn't want me going."

"What! Really? But wait a sec, aren't you two on a break of some sort?"

"We are, or well, I thought we were. I didn't expect that he would be so. . .demanding over me," she confessed.

"He sounds jealous. Especially as it's with superstar Sam Balfer," Paisley said with a bubbly voice.

"It's just a date, I'll be there for the launch of his latest movie, and his publicist thinks it's a good idea for him to have a friend as his 'date'," she explained. When she explained it, it didn't seem so bad. But when you included emotions, no wonder Mike had flipped.

"Is sex on the agenda?" Paisley chuckled.

I wish. "No, just a date, you cheeky girl." She knew Paisley was being silly but wondered if Mike was genuinely worried that she'd sleep with Sam. "I don't know what to do. Do I go and have a wonderful night knowing there's no chance of Mike and I getting back together? That's assuming I want to. Or cancel with Sam?"

There was a pause, and Paige knew her sister was thinking. She was the one who didn't make hasty decisions. She was methodical in her decision making, and the perfect choice for helping her out today.

"That's a tough one," she finally said.

It was. And Paige was still unsure what to do.

The baby gurgled in the background reminding Paige that she was taking her sister away from some precious moments she had with her son. "Can I ask? If you knew then what you know now, would you have kept your pregnancy a secret? Doesn't Lev have a right to have a father?"

She heard Paisley sigh. "That's a twenty-million-dollar question, and I can't answer that. I made a decision with what I knew at the time. You know how it was between the two of us. And the fall-out after. I tried to fix it. It didn't work."

"Sorry, I didn't mean to upset you," she said with genuine remorse, staring at the carpet.

"It's okay. You've been the most amazing, supportive sister, I don't know what I would've done without you." She paused. "My advice is that you can only make tough decisions with the knowledge around you. You know that Mike is not happy about the date. You want to go. You have to decide which is more important, Mike? Sam?"

Paige let out a heavy sigh of regret.

"Pretend that he'll want nothing to do with you if

you go out with Sam. And then make your decision," her sister suggested.

Like Paisley, Paige had also been so surprised at Mike's reaction. She knew he wasn't going to be happy about it, but not as seething as he'd been. "Sam is my celebrity pass, which is why I think he believes we're going to have sex." She confessed with a knotted belly. "Between us, it's not going to happen. He was always a really nice guy. But, you know, he may not even remember me. It's not like we've been in regular contact since he left Australia when he was eighteen."

Paisley sighed. "I don't know what to say. This is such a difficult situation. I will tell you that there are times I question my decisions, but it's too late. It's done." She cleared her throat. "If you think Mike is the one for you and you don't want to lose him, then cancel the date. Don't miss your chance at love. That's probably the best advice I can give you."

Paisley's advice didn't help, mainly because she didn't know if Mike was the guy for her. Did she see him long term? Was he the one she wanted to have kids with? Would he want to take their child to the park? Because if she knew the answers then she wouldn't have asked for some thinking time. . .would she?

Her shoulder drooped with the decision she

needed to make. "Thanks, Pais. Give my nephew a kiss from me, I'll see you soon, okay?"

"Will do, love you," her sister replied in her usual happy voice.

"Love you right back," she said before disconnecting the call.

Paisley had made a difficult decision, and was now a single mum. But her sister had remained positive and hopeful despite it. Her sister lived in the moment. She'd made a decision about Lev, and accepted it. Things had changed since. And the same had to be done for her.

She needed to look at the facts and make the decision based on them.

She was twenty-nine, not ninety-nine. Time to live, just like Paisley had done.

A sense of calm settled over her, and she stretched her arms over her head, feeling the cricks ease out of her spine.

The decision was made...

SAM BALFER CLOSED his eyes and leaned back into the plush leather seats of the SUV. Despite flying first class and sleeping most of the long flight from LA to Melbourne, he was tired and cranky.

Megan, his assistant, sat beside him discussing his schedule for the next week. He lifted his hand. "There better be time for me to see my parents," he snapped at her.

"Of course," she said, ignoring his bad temperament. "You're seeing them today."

She continued talking, and even though his eyes were still closed he listened to everything she'd organised. Meticulous, efficient, and hard working. Megan organised his life and ensured his privacy was respected.

When she'd finished he turned to her. "You've done a good job. Sorry for snapping at you."

Looking immaculate, as though she hadn't been travelling for a day, she gave him her usual smile. "It's fine." She paused. "Tonight, we have the premiere of *Homecoming*, and you'll be happy to know that it's not black tie."

"Thank goodness," he said with relief. He wasn't in the mood for a formal event, and he was hoping to leave the premiere as early as possible.

"It's a more casual event, so you can wear dark jeans and a jacket," she continued, "And, your date tonight is one of your friends?"

He straightened and his heart lifted. "Who?"

"Paige Dalton," she read from her screen.

"Paige," he said with a sigh. "Did you know we went to school together?"

His assistant nodded, appearing not to be too interested in her.

He leaned back into the seat and thought about Paige. Paige, his high school friend who'd helped him with grades. She was so smart and he was sure she'd be working in cancer research or molecular biology or something he didn't understand.

He smiled thinking about the two of them hanging out with friends on St Kilda beach, eating fish and chips. Too often he was working or auditioning for some ad or TV show. But over the school vacations and weekends, the highlight of his teen years was being with Paige, and his friends.

It took him twelve years of modelling and acting to become the overnight success he was at age eighteen. And only his friends, especially Paige, understood that.

He couldn't wait to see her.

He turned to Megan and said with gratitude, "Good work, thanks for organising Paige."

IT WAS TUESDAY AFTERNOON, and in a few hours, she'd be seeing Sam for the first time in years. Her hands were shaking, and she'd gone to the toilet six times in the past two hours.

Her cousin, Jasmine, and her best friend, Lola, had assured her they'd bought her the perfect outfit for her to wear as they styled her hair and applied makeup.

"Please don't go overboard, you know I don't wear much makeup," she instructed Lola as her palms went from clammy, to cold, to clammy again.

She caught Lola giving Jas a cheeky wink. Since they'd arrived, she'd felt that there was a joke that everyone was laughing about. . .except her.

"Are you laughing at me?" She directed at Lola, her hands twisting in her lap.

"No, not at all." Lola gave her shoulder a reassuring squeeze. "We're very excited for you." She held up her hand. "I promise."

A secret look passed between the two friends that was obviously supposed to be private, but was seen by her. "What's going on, you two?"

"Nothing, I promise," Lola said in a reassuring voice, that did little to reassure her.

They finished with a flourish, and an admiration for their work.

"Look how you good you look," Jasmine said passing a hand mirror to her.

Paige admired the makeup they'd applied. Not

overly done and she looked good. "Thank you, I love it."

"Time to get dressed." Jas lifted the large paper bag she'd brought. "And don't worry, we didn't get you high heels, since you only wear runners. Check out these ankle boots." She lifted them from the bag, and Paige was impressed.

"Perfect," Paige massaged her heart with her palm.

"They are, the heel is not high, but they are super sexy," Lola announced.

"You've both been so thoughtful, I love what you've done so far," Paige said as her trembling fingers reached for the bag of clothes. "Okay. Time to get dressed, let's see how I look."

A few minutes later, standing in front of the mirror, she stared at her reflection. Giddy with relief, she admired the outfit selected for her. With her hair styled, and makeup applied, she looked very different from the studious engineer that she was.

She'd even removed her glasses, and was wearing contact lenses for the evening. Something she rarely did.

The lenses were comfortable and easy to wear. She just hid behind her glasses, because she'd been doing it since high school. Very childish indeed.

"We've gone for a sexy rocker look, you like?" Lola asked, full of expectation.

She looked at their faces, and could see concern in their widened eyes.

Jasmine wet her lips with her tongue. "Please don't tell us you hate it, you look ah-maz-ing."

Paige turned around, admiring herself from behind before she turned to face them. "No, I like it, I like it a lot," she said slowly, still unable to believe how well they'd dressed her up. "I've never worn such tight pants before."

"With your height, you should," Lola reassured her.

In skin-tight black leather-look pants, they'd teamed a black singlet, chunky gold necklace and draped a cropped leather-look jacket over. It was dark, sexy and alluring, all in one amazing look. Apart from mascara and powder, the emphasis of her makeup was deep red lips. Redder than red.

She drew a steady breath, admiring how different she looked from the casual jeans and T-shirts she favoured. "I still can't believe how good I look."

"You look hot. And if you'd gotten yourself out of your boring jeans and T-shirts sooner, you'd see how fab you can look." Jas admonished her with a waggle of her finger, and a grin. "Not many women can wear those pants. They make your legs and butt look sexy."

Sexy? She didn't think so. But she had to admit, they'd done a really good job in making her look good.

"We've got plenty of time to get to the hotel, but let's take some pics of you," Lola said, tugging her mobile phone from her pocket.

Her forehead creased with curiosity. "What do you mean *we* have plenty of time? There's no *we*."

Jasmine gave her a warm smile. "Do you think we'd leave you on your own? You're so nervous that my tummy is rolling in sympathy for you."

The three of them chuckled.

"You've both taken time off work to buy me an outfit and dress me up," she started to say but stopped when they both crossed their arms and fired an *I can't believe you're saying that* look at her.

"Don't worry, we won't ruin your moment with Sam. We'll get you to the hotel, and then fade to the background," Lola said with a toss of her hair.

She eyed the two best friends, her gaze taking in their flawless makeup, perfectly styled hair, and knock-out figures. "You two could never *fade* into the background," she said with a grin.

"Too right." Jasmine sang out. "But for you, we will." She gave her a wink.

"We want to make sure your date, tonight, is the best it can be," Lola said with a flourish of her hand.

"I doubt Sam will see it as anything more than a catch-up with a school friend. But for me. . .it will be very, very special," she confessed in a low voice. Because it was special.

THE THREE OF them made their way to the five-star hotel in Melbourne CBD where Sam was staying.

Any moment, Paige was waiting for a camera crew to jump out and shout *gotcha*, *fooled you*, or something as upsetting as that.

She was an engineer whose life revolved around her family and her friends. She shunned the spotlight, and preferred quiet nights at home rather than clubbing.

Her date tonight with a world-wide celebrity still seemed surreal to her, not possible. There were times she wondered if the publicist in LA was real.

"I wish Rachel was here," she sighed as they walked through the lobby. Not having her BFF with her on one of the most important days of her life was like having a knife wedged in her ribs. "It was Rachel that made this all possible."

"We're not," Jassy laughed. "If she was here, we'd miss out."

Paige nodded. Rachel was her best friend, the one who'd organised everything, and used her savings on *her*. But Rachel's manager had one of her regular meltdowns insisting that Rachel was needed at work. Her leave application had been refused, and both Rachel and Paige had been devastated.

The "hand-holding" and support had fallen to Jasmine and Lola. She may not be as close to them as she was to Rachel, but at least they were both competent, and had helped her so much this afternoon.

Their stiletto heels clattered on the polished tiles, and Paige's anxiety hit a new level making her feel nauseous. She may look like a sexy rocker chick, but on the inside, she was just her. The smart sister, with a high IQ, who'd successfully completed her degree with a high distinction.

"You'll be fine," Jasmine reassured her, as though reading her thoughts.

Jasmine's calm manner did little to quell the nerves rolling in her belly. She was about to meet Sam now that he was one of Hollywood's most in-demand actors. It didn't matter that they went to school together, their lives were so very different now.

The lady who greeted them in the lobby intro-duced herself as Megan Berry. She had long, dark hair which shone under the hotel lights, and wore a tailored outfit that screamed designer. She was tapping her heels and had the look of someone who was extremely busy. "You're finally here," she said with an exasperated sigh. "Follow me."

Paige rolled her eyes. They were five minutes *early*.

Walking in high heels at a speed that would impress a marathon runner, Megan walked away from them, and they followed. Within moments they were in a lift heading skyward. Megan's gaze took in her rocker outfit and Paige squirmed in her new boots. She felt out of sorts. Did she know that her friends had not only dressed her but styled her? Was it that obvious?

"You brought a *support* team with you?" She mocked, giving Lola and Jasmine a narrowed look. "You two aren't coming in," she said with a toss of her perfectly coifed hair.

Megan's focus then returned to her mobile phone and her thumbs busily replied to a message.

Then the lift doors opened, and the four of them stepped out. "Ladies." She pointed a manicured finger to the elevator.

Jas and Lola gave Paige a quick hug before diligently retreating, under the watchful eye of Megan, back into the lift.

The doors closed and Megan turned to her. She would've been the same age as Paige, but her demeanour told her she was not someone to mess with. "My job is to keep Sam managed. I'm his executive assistant and I don't have time to deal with semantics and broken hearts. This is the premier of Sam's new movie, *Homecoming*. We have a lot riding on it, and it's my job to make sure that everything runs efficiently." She gave her a smile that reminded Paige of a tiger that was about to eat its prey. "Your job is to smile and look pretty, that's it. Don't embarrass him. Don't upset him. Don't talk to the press." She paused. "Under no circumstances are you to talk to the press or anyone else about Sam. You signed an NDA, and we will sue you if we hear that you've broken it." She gave her a sickly-sweet smile.

Paige nodded. She'd read every word of the agreement, and knew the expectations. If her tummy was in knots before, she was even more nervous now, if that was possible. They made their way down a carpeted hallway, the sounds of Megan's heels muffled by the thick wool shag. They approached a door guarded by a large security guard. He nodded at them, and then opened the door, allowing them through before closing it again.

Paige's eyes widened at the sight of the beautiful suite. Sam would stay in a beautiful room, of course, but this suite took her breath away. With sweeping views of the city and exquisite styling, Paige's jaw dropped and her mouth resembled a goldfish.

She snapped it shut.

Megan turned to her. "Cell phone please." She held out her palm and Paige dutifully placed her phone in it. "You'll get it back later. Wait here," she instructed.

Paige made her way to the window and looked out. She couldn't sit. She couldn't eat. She couldn't check her phone. The enormity of what was about to happen cloaked her as heavily as a winter jacket. Her breathing was laboured and she was so anxious that her hands started to shake.

She took five long, steady breaths to calm her heart rate, and then she counted backwards from ten to one. It did little to quell the nervousness in her belly. A noise made her look up, and in walked Sam. The air whooshed out of her lungs as he strode towards her. His full lips upturned in a welcoming smile that made her feel warm and fuzzy inside.

"Paige," he said, "I'm so happy to see you." He pulled her into an embrace.

Her arms went around his slim waist, as she hugged him back...tightly. "It's good to see you, too," she said. Unable to help herself, she breathed in the sexy scent of his aftershave and gorgeousness.

Taking a step back he said, "You look fantastic." He led her to a nearby sofa and they sat, facing each other. "How are you?"

"Well," she replied, "Really well. But look at you, Mr Hollywood Star."

He chuckled at her joke and she took a moment to admire his dark hair, styled to look like he'd just got out of bed. That sexy, alluring look would've taken time and had been achieved by a professional stylist but it made him look even sexier. He was dressed casually in an outfit that complimented hers, dark jeans, black tee, and black leather jacket.

"Tell me, Paige, about yourself. Did you become a scientist like you always wanted to be?" He rubbed his chin. "I lost contact with most of my friends when I moved to LA." He let out a long breath. "God, the work. The hours. It just makes friends and relationships so much harder. Forget me, I'm interested in *you*. Tell me what you do."

She felt herself blush under the intense gaze of his dark eyes. She did like that he'd remembered her career plans from when they were at school. "I work at a large company as a Structural Engineer. I became an engineer, not a scientist. I love my career, and the company I work for."

Megan walked in. "We need to go now," she said, killing any further conversation.

He stood and helped her to her feet. "I really want us to catch up and spend time together, but we need to go soon. We'll talk more after?"

"Of course," she replied with a smile. *As if she'd say no.*

Hotel security took her, Sam, Megan, and a few others via the back elevator to the car park. A large black limousine was waiting for them, the tinted windows didn't allow her to see in.

A driver stood at the car door, holding it open.

"After you," Sam said.

Seated next to each other Paige tried to relax in the black leather softness but she couldn't. She was on her way to the world premiere of a new movie with Sam as her date. She leaned over and whispered in his ear. "Can I ask a big favour?"

He looked at her. "Sure."

"Would you take a selfie of us? Otherwise, it's like this night didn't happen," she said in a low voice. She wanted a physical memento of their night together. Something just for her, that would not be shown to anyone. . .except Rachel and Paisley.

He stifled a chuckle. "Megan confiscated your phone?"

She nodded.

He rolled his eyes before tugging his phone out from his pocket. Forgetting the others were in the car with them, she focussed on the photos of them, cheeks pressed together as they looked at the camera.

"Thanks," she said, before reading out her number so he could send a copy to her. "It's just for me, I promise I won't circulate it."

He winked at her. "I trust you."

And that's when her stomach went into freefall. One of the sexiest guys on the planet had winked at her, taken a selfie with her, and was her date for the night. OH. EM. GEE.

It seemed that a dozen conversations were happening in the limo at the same time around her.

Megan ensured there would be no further whispers between them as she went through a checklist. Directing her gaze to Sam she said, "You know what to do. Smile, sign autographs, pose for selfies."

Megan then turned to look at her, giving her a look that would impress a school principal dealing with unruly children. "Keep out of Sam's way when he's having photos with fans. You can appear next to him for the press, and if they ask you to move, then move. If they ask who you are, you say you're a friend."

Paige wanted to remind her that she been told not to talk to the press. She also decided not to salute Megan, even though the words fired at her made her want to.

Within minutes, the limo arrived at the movie cinema and she bit her lip to stop it from trembling. It seemed Sam had noticed her nerves and he took her hand and held it in his warm one. "It's okay," he whispered in her ear.

She tried to give him a reassuring smile, but it was difficult with her heart galloping so hard she expected it to burst from the confinements of her rib cage.

Megan turned to her, again, giving her a cold glare. "This is the worldwide premiere of Sam's new movie. Don't ruin this for him."

Her nerves were already shot to pieces so she really didn't appreciate Megan's words. Megan may have Sam's interests at heart, but she wasn't stupid enough to spoil this for him. Biting back a retort, she appreciated Sam's warm smile and encouragement.

She nodded. Her throat was so dry that even swallowing hurt, like she'd eaten a box of razor blades.

A noise made her look at the window and Paige's eyes widened at the sight of hundreds of screaming women, all calling out Sam's name. "It certainly seems you've become a bigger star since your soap opera days," she said.

He chuckled. "Let's do this."

The door was opened, and Paige could see a sea of mobile phones held high, in upstretched arms, as fans tried to capture images of Sam's arrival.

Sam was being called to as people vied for his attention.

He alighted from the car, then turned to help her out.

Behind her, Megan called out, "Make sure you smile."

Great advice, she thought. Like she didn't know she had to do that.

Feeling anxious, nervous and excited, she clutched Sam's hand for safety as they walked down a red carpet surrounded by screaming fans. Her daydream of being with the guy she'd had a crush on for years was now a reality. Despite her nerves, she intended on enjoying every minute of it. Because, like Cinderella, eventually, everything would go back to normal. Sam would return to his exciting life in LA while she'd continue her mundane life in Melbourne. . .and tonight would be just a treasured memory.

CHAPTER 4

*W*hat started as terrifying turned out to be the highlight of her inconsequential 29 years. Unlike her three sisters, Paige was quiet. She preferred nights at home, playing board games, reading, and watching movies. But for *one* night, Paige was the star. She was treated like she was famous. And as much as she hated to admit it, she loved every second of it.

The press loved her being Sam's date, a childhood friend. Any questions were competently managed by Megan. Paige couldn't wipe the smile off her face even if she wanted to. She waved at fans and smiled non-stop. It was fun to be the centre of attention and liked by everyone.

She was the nerdy sister, the smart one, and until now it'd never bothered her that she wasn't as pretty as her three sisters. She was the eldest, the most forthright but underneath that strong exterior was a woman who still wanted to be accepted. And that was the problem with Mike—she'd started dating him for all the wrong reasons. She just hadn't realised. . .till now.

"Having fun?" asked Sam, interrupting her thoughts.

"Yes," she said. "so much, no wonder you love this life."

"It has its ups and downs," Sam said with a pensive look in his eyes.

They were now inside the cinema complex, surrounded by beautiful people wearing stylish outfits, that were completely beyond Paige's spend limit. She'd been fortunate that Jasmine and Lola had found her clothes from a factory outlet sale.

Sam handed her a glass of champagne, then leaned forward to whisper in her ear. "We're not staying for the movie."

Her face fell. She'd been so looking forward to seeing his new movie. "We're not?"

"You think I want to waste two hours watching *myself* on-screen when I could be spending time with you?"

Paige sucked in a deep breath and every skin cell tingled with anticipation. "You want to spend time with me?" Holy smokes, a night with Sam! There was little that could keep her from spending time with him. Perhaps a family emergency? But it'd have to be a mighty large one.

His lips turned into a warm smile. The same smile that had graced hundreds of magazine covers and had made him a star.

Her fingers fluttered to her throat. "How could I say no to that?" She paused. "I guess, I can see the movie tomorrow night." She gave him a cheeky wink as her heart rate quickened. She'd flirted with Sam. A first for her.

His arm came around her waist, and he drew her near. The warmth of his touch seared through the material of her skin-tight pants.

"Let's get out of here," he said, before tugging her away from the crowds.

WHAT HAD STARTED AS A CASUAL, throwaway line to Megan weeks ago had eventuated into a night of possibilities, Sam thought. He'd made a joke that his date for the night should be a friend to help promote his movie. He hadn't expected it to happen. It seemed absurd at the time and he hadn't thought about it again until Megan had told him it was all organised.

Seeing Paige for the first time in over ten years had shaken him to such a point that he was filled with wistfulness, yearning, and nostalgia. How had so much time passed? He hadn't realised how much he'd missed his friends and his life in Australia till Paige had walked back into his life.

He'd left Australia when he was eighteen, with stars in his eyes, clutching a contract, bound for Hollywood, and hadn't looked back since.

He'd been living in LA for twelve years now, and his life revolved around his work. The people he saw, the people he interacted with, and the people he socialised with, were actors or worked with actors. He hadn't had time to miss his friends because he'd been so busy working. His social media was handled by an assistant, and he hadn't realised how much of a social bubble he'd been living in until this moment.

While his career had exploded and he lived in LA, his Melbourne friends had continued their lives here in Melbourne... but now he wanted to find out what they were up to and what he had missed.

In an outfit that screamed "sexy", Paige looked very different from how he remembered her. At school her face had been clean and free of makeup, and her hair was always brushed into a neat pony-tail. Gone were the thick glasses and bashful blushes.

The woman he'd been confronted with was gorgeous. He hadn't been expecting her to have been dressed head to toe in black with fiery red lipstick.

He'd been impressed that she'd accepted Megan's demands without a fuss, not all his dates had wanted to give up their cells. And he liked that she seemed genuinely excited at the opening tonight.

He'd seen the disappointment in her eyes when he told her they were leaving early but, honestly, he was not interested in wasting two hours watching a movie he'd spent four months working on.

Only his security details and Megan knew of his plans, and he steered Paige towards a side door. "Come this way," he directed.

Walking with haste, he was almost pulling her along, through a number of corridors before coming out into the dark night. The limo was waiting for them and they went in before either the media or fans recognised them.

"Sorry about the sharp exit, I just wanted to get out of there," he confessed.

"You didn't check with me," she replied, with a pout. Her lips twitched which made him think she wasn't that worried about leaving.

The luxurious car started to move, and the closed windows gave them privacy. It reminded him of the bubble existence of his life.

"I know I seem ungrateful since I was your date for tonight, but I just, um, I just didn't want to leave early." She cleared her throat as though embarrassed at what she was telling him. "I've never experienced anything like tonight." She paused and gave him a smile. "What a rush to have everyone fawn over you like that."

"I'm used to it," he confessed. He was genuinely surprised that she wanted to stay. He remembered her being withdrawn and not very social.

"This is my first and last time I'll ever get to be a star or rather be famous, because I know you." She made quotation marks in the air when she said famous. "It was my fifteen minutes of fame. Instead of being Phoebe's sister, or the sister with the degrees, or the one who. . .doesn't matter." She shrugged. "It looks like I'll now be known as *that friend* of Sam Balfer's."

"Is that what you want?" he asked, curious to know more. He'd encountered enough wannabes who tried to use him to leverage their careers. Pathetic really.

She raised her eyebrow skyward. "I'm still the shy nerdy girl you knew from school. The difference is that I now have an honours degree and an excellent job. I think the new outfit gave me the boost of confidence I needed tonight."

"Well, you look great. And besides, I'm sure you're more than your work," he said, rubbing his jaw.

"From the guy who I went to school with, who now rubs shoulders with Hollywood's elite." She chuckled. "I don't think so."

"May I make it up to you?" He hoped she would like the surprise he'd organised. He'd been genuinely excited to hear who his date was. Usually, he was teamed up with an up-and-coming actor or model, but Paige? A friend from school? He was more than keen.

"Sure, why not," she said.

"We'll go out for dinner, and reminisce." He lifted the handset and spoke to the driver. "Take us to St. Kilda." The beachside suburb where they'd spent many hours on weekends, and school vacations.

"Yes, Mr Balfer," came the reply.

He replaced the handset and looked at her.

A smile stretched her lips. "You're taking me to St. Kilda?" She gasped, having made the connection. "Surely you don't mean…"

He resisted the urge to punch the air, delighted she remembered. "Yep, I'm taking you out for fish and chips."

She placed her hands over her heart and cooed. "You haven't forgotten." Her forehead then creased, as though suddenly recalling something important. "Hang on a minute, you're just going to walk in? You? The movie star?"

He rolled his eyes, pretending to be offended. "You think nothing is organised." His hand brushed away her concerns with a dismissive wave. "I value my privacy too much."

She gave him a large grin.

"To Leo's it is," he said.

"To Leo's." Her voice sang out, with joy, in the car.

TEN MINUTES later the limousine pulled up outside the small diner and the security guard opened the door, helping them out.

"If you want to remain inconspicuous, you probably shouldn't arrive at a fast food restaurant in a limo," she chuckled, still unable to believe that she was out with Sam, going to their favourite diner... from all those years ago. She wished she had her phone with her so she could capture the moment with another photo. But alas, everything would be stored and treasured in her memory.

"Well, yes, you're right. Unfortunately, I can't

walk around the streets like everyone else, anymore," he remarked with a decisive nod.

"Do you miss that?" She couldn't imagine what it would be like to lose your privacy and not be able to enjoy any spontaneity in your life.

He nodded. "More than I thought I would." There was a visible swallow. A moment that she thought there was some regret. And then it was gone. The smile he gave her said acceptance. He enjoyed his life and fully connected to his acting world.

Holding the door open for her, they walked in and found a solitary table in the middle of the diner, set for two. Sheets were stuck to the window, blocking the outside world, giving them privacy and preventing onlookers from seeing in through the large glass windows.

Everything was still the same as when they were teens, from the menu board to the plastic chairs and tables.

"Everything is as I remembered," he said in the low voice as his gaze took in the 1970s décor.

She nudged him with delight. "The menu hasn't changed much," she pointed to the board above the deep fryers.

He turned to her with a mischievous look in his eye. "They've just updated the prices."

They chuckled, bonding over shared memories,

each remembering the times they'd spent here all those years ago. She'd loved every minute, as a teen, they'd spent on the foreshore. Whether alone or with friends, being with Sam, enjoying his company had been the highlight of her school years.

A young man with a wide grin approached them. "Good evening. What can I get you?"

"Um, I was just wondering, if um, Leo still works here?" she asked, her voice was filled with excitement and anticipation.

"Leo is my dad," the man said with a cheerful smile. "But he's currently overseas on a cruise. If he'd known you'd be here tonight"—he looked directly at Sam—"he would've made sure he was here." He pointed to the lone table. "Everything is as you requested."

"Thank you," Sam said before turning to look at her. "Fish and chips?"

"That sounds great," she said as warmth spread through her body. The unexpected detour of coming to Leo's had excited her and filled her with such elation that she was surprised she hadn't broken out into a song and started dancing around the room.

"Why don't you two take a seat, and I'll organise dinner. Won't be too long," the owner's son said.

The young man was trying to hide his excitement, but she could see the sparkle in his eyes, knowing that he had one of Hollywood's best eating in his diner. It wasn't every day that Sam Balfer turned up and ordered fish and chips.

Trying not to look too eager or overly excited, she pressed her lips together and counted to five. She could do this. All she needed to do was remind herself that she was with her teen friend, not some hot shot that made her heart sigh every time he smiled at her.

They each grabbed a bottle of water from the fridge and sat down on the worn white plastic chairs, facing each other.

A serious look crossed his eyes before he took a big sip of water. Looking directly at her, he asked, "Would you have preferred to go somewhere more classy? Fancier?"

Paige would've laughed if she hadn't seen the concern in his eyes. "Of course not, this place is perfect. I haven't been here for ages and it's really nice to come back here with *you*." She paused. "I have to confess I'm very excited and happy to be here with you."

His eyes lit up, and she could tell he was happy and relieved for the choices he'd made. "When I knew I was coming back to Melbourne, I wanted to come *here* and see if the food is as good as I remembered it."

She lifted her eyebrow, teasing him. "So, what do you think? Do you think it will be as good?" It had to be. Melbourne was full of excellent restaurants and cafes; it was a foodie haven. For a local diner to still be around all those years, it had to have been making quality food.

He looked at her, with his dark eyes filled with pensive thoughts. "I hope so." He lifted his water bottle and toasted her. "To a most memorable evening."

Elation radiated through her body as she lifted her plastic bottle and touched it against his. "Cheers."

He drank half the bottle of water before leaning back in his chair. "Tell me about yourself and your sisters. Your names all start with P, but you never did tell me why." He leaned forward. "Do you want to tell me why, *now?*"

His deep voice made her toes curl in her boots, and she felt her cheeks warm under his intense gaze. "That's what you want to know?"

"It's something I've always wanted to know and you'd never tell me," he said with a nostalgic look.

"Well," she said with a wince. "It's embarrassing." There was a reason she hadn't told him then. Only her bestie, Rachel, knew the truth. Her parents may think the reason was cute and adorable, but they were the parents.

"You think I don't understand embarrassing? You've seen how many articles have been written about me, do you think they were all true?" he said with a wave of his hand in the air.

Yep, she knew how much had been written about him. She'd read many of them. "Touché," she said. She rubbed the back of her neck, knowing she was stalling but she was out on a date with Sam, and he wanted to know about her and her sisters. Feeling slightly lightheaded, she said, "You've probably heard more embarrassing stories than mine; it's just that... my parents are so—"

"They love you, there's nothing to be embarrassed about," he added.

It wasn't the love she was embarrassed about. It was all the things they did, had done over the years that she preferred to keep "in the family." She gave him a dramatic sigh. "Okay, I'll tell you. Dad wanted all of us to have names that began with the letter P."

"P for?" His frown gave away his impatience for her not telling him straight away.

She bit her lip. "Promise me you won't laugh?"

He raised his hand, palm up. "Scouts honour." His voice was filled with honesty, as was the look in his eyes. She could trust him; he wouldn't repeat what she was about to confess.

Taking a deep breath, she said, "P is for Princess. That's right, to him, we were all his princesses." She rolled her eyes with faux irritation. "And so, we all got names that began with P. Paige. Poppy. Phoebe. Paisley."

He chuckled with amusement. "That's it?"

"That's it," she said with a bright smile.

"That's sweet of your dad," he said, and she could see genuine joy in his smile. "I remember Poppy," he announced.

Poppy. Her gorgeous, crazy sister who seemed to love dogs more than people...apart from her family. "She's two years younger than me, but we were only separated by one school year."

"And the other two?"

"Paisley and Phoebe are twins, they're 23."

"Yes, they were much younger than us, but I remember meeting them at your home when you tutored me. Paisley was so studious and Phoebe, well, she was always doing some sort of performance."

"She loves the limelight, and thrives on being the centre of attention," she added, remembering all the times she interrupted her and Sam studying. It was the start of their love/hate relationship, which eased once Phoebe moved overseas.

As much as she loved her younger sister, she was privately jealous of her ability to light up a room, simply by walking into it. Only Phoebe, of the four sisters, had the confidence to strut around in a tiny bikini on a stage.

"Lucky for me, *you* were my friend. I couldn't have got through high school without your help," he said. "I missed so many classes thanks to all those auditions."

Her hands tingled in response to his compliment. She may no longer blush, like she did in high school, at the mention of his name. But he still had the ability to make her hormones cartwheel in excitement. "Well, you can thank me *now* and buy me dinner," she said with a cheeky wink.

"It will be my pleasure." His joyous smile made her tummy tumble, just like it had all those years ago.

A young man brought their food to the table, interrupting them. "Here you go." He placed a large package, wrapped in paper, in the middle of the table with a bottle of ketchup. "Enjoy."

She eyed it, the smell of salt and fish filled her nostrils and her tummy growled in appreciation. Thanks to her nerves, she'd barely eaten all day.

"They still serve their food wrapped in butcher's paper," she said, pointing to it.

"The only difference is that we're eating in here and not outside on the beach," he added. "Remember how good it was to sit, eat chips and watch the tide roll in and out?"

"Good times," she said. "This feels fancy, sitting at the table eating." She unwrapped their dinner from the white paper. "It smells delicious."

The pile of fried food was between them, and she sprinkled extra salt over the chips, remembering how he liked that.

"My mouth is watering, I don't remember the last time I had fries." He paused. "Don't tell my trainer I ate here," he said with a wink.

"Your secret is safe with me," she replied, tapping her nose like there was a conspiracy.

The dinner consisted of enough fries to feed an army, fried potato cakes, and several pieces of golden, battered fish. Heavenly. She squeezed a generous dollop of ketchup on the side before eating a couple of fries. "Still perfect."

They ate, the conversation restricted to comments regarding their food. And when they'd eaten to the bursting point, Sam leaned back in his seat. "That was so good."

She finished a bottle of water and grabbed a

couple more from the fridge handing one to him. She said opposite him, still quite unable to believe she was having dinner with one of Hollywood's most eligible bachelors. "Tell me what it's like in LA? Do you like living there? Do you miss Melbourne?"

"It's busier than Melbourne but yeah, I like it, it's home now." He paused, reflecting on his words. "I can't believe I just said that," he confessed. "I have a nice house, staff to manage it, staff to manage me, and I'm working a job that I love. I couldn't do that here."

"You've just answered my next question," she said. "I want to know if you're happy, and you are. You're one of the lucky ones. Not only did you get an amazing break when you were young, you've been working steadily ever since."

"You know that luck is only 5% of achievement. I've been working since I can remember. All those ads, local theatre, and soapies. When all my friends were having fun, I was either acting, learning how to act or studying." His hand cupped his chin as he reminisced.

"But you were working on that big blockbuster movie when you were 18, surely there was luck in you getting *that* role?" She beamed with certainty.

He'd had a minor role in a large American movie

that was being filmed in Australia. At the end of the filming, he'd been signed up with one of Hollywood's most reputable studios and left Melbourne to live in America. Paige had been so happy and proud of him but a piece of her heart had died that day, knowing their friendship would never be the same. From that one successful movie, he'd starred in dozens more.

His elbows rested on the table and his fingers pressed together, creating a steeple. "It's a ruthless business, everyone wants to be a star. You know almost everyone in LA is an actor."

"I've been impressed with what you've achieved," she admitted in a low voice. "Tell me about your latest? *Homecoming?*"

"I've enjoyed all the movies I've done so far, most have been dramas and some historicals, as you know. But my agent was approached with this romantic comedy. It's not usually what I do, but I read the script and really liked it. I had a lot of fun working with the cast and crew of *Homecoming.*"

"Did you fall for your co-star?" She waggled her eyebrows. "Isn't that what's supposed to happen? The leads fall in love or have an affair?"

He shrugged with indifference. "It happens... but not with me. Kate's not my type."

She fiddled with the water bottle wanting to

know more and also dreading it. "What's your type... if you don't mind me asking."

He whistled through his teeth. "You ask the hard questions, sure you're not a reporter?"

She placed her hand on her heart, and raised the other one, palm facing him. "Promise."

"Don't get me wrong, I loved working with Kate. She's incredibly talented and fun to be with." He took a deep breath. "She just doesn't make my heart race."

She wasn't expecting that his definition of love would be romantic. "Is that what love is to you? That when you meet that someone special, she will make your heart race?"

A quizzical look crossed his eyes before he sat straighter, as if it was important that he clarify his position on love to her. "If there's no spark to start with, you can't create one."

She nodded.

He blew out a long breath. "Falling in love on set is not for me. It's not realistic. You're living in a bubble." His hands made a circular shape in the air. "And when you come out of it, things are different in real life than how things were on set."

Her lips parted as she mulled over what he'd just said. "That makes sense."

"My turn to ask." He looked directly at her. "Do

you have someone special? Is there a bloke who cares that you're out with me tonight?"

Paige felt her throat swell and then swell some more. She drained her bottle of water and seeing her hands shake slightly, she then screwed the top back onto the bottle and placed her hands in her lap. She should say no, flutter her eyelashes and move on. Because that's what Phoebe would do. But she wasn't Phoebe. She was the quiet, geeky sister. She was the one that had no idea what to do, the sister who could count the number of boyfriends she'd had on one hand.

The clothes had given her confidence, but underneath she was just an engineer who liked to skateboard and hang out with her friends. If she told Sam the truth, he'd think she was a complete and utter loser. So she made a split-second decision to tell him a *half* truth, that way it didn't feel like lying.

She pasted on a smile to hide the muscles in her cheeks that were quivering with nerves. "We were friends at school but things are different now. You're world-famous, you have staff to look after you and security." Her head nodded towards the large beefy man who stood at the front door, and knowing another still on the other side of the front door at the street. "I'm just an everyday gal trying to fit into your world for one night."

He scratched his chin. "You know, you've done a very good job deflecting my question. I'll ask again, are you seeing someone?"

Her breathing hitched. She wanted to tell him the truth, she really did. She wanted to be sassy and say something like, *do you know that you are my celebrity pass* with a lift of her eyebrow. But there's no way she was gonna say that. So instead she took a deep breath to reassure herself and admitted, "Sort of."

His forehead creased and so did the skin between his eyebrows. "How do you have a *sort of* boyfriend?" He looked at her and under his watchful gaze, she felt herself squirm in her new boots.

She rubbed her moist palms up and down her fake leather pants. "We've been together for a few months but a couple of weeks ago, I suggested a break." She blew out a long breath. "His idea of a break is different from mine."

"And?"

"Let's just say that Mike wasn't too happy about tonight."

And wasn't that the understatement of the year?

CHAPTER 5

*P*aige felt herself go hot then cold. Why were they talking about Mike? And why couldn't they get back to the safer subjects...like the weather? Or one of her sisters?

"Tell me." His softened tone demanded a response, he was curious and wanted to know more.

She gazed into his dark eyes, mesmerised by them, just as she had been in high school. Her heart hammered against her chest and her mouth dried as though she'd been drinking sand, rather than cool water.

His brow furrowed with concern and then released. "Paige, if he's going to cause issues, Megan needs to know about it."

She shook her head as embarrassment made her squirm in her seat. "Mike's not going to go to the press or do anything to affect you, he just didn't want me having sex with you." The truth rolled off her tongue and as soon as she said it, her hands flew up and covered her mouth. "Ohmygad, I can't believe I just told you that."

Sam threw back his head and laughed. And she wished the tiled floor would sink and swallow her whole.

"I'd been seeing Mike for a few months."

"And it's serious?"

"For him perhaps." She winced, really not wanting to have this conversation with Sam. Biting her lip and pretending he wasn't one of Hollywood's best actors, and she didn't have a massive crush on him, she said, "Um, he's nice and I enjoy being with him but when he suggested I move in with him, I asked for a break."

"Ouch," he said.

"I know. He still calls me, and treats me like we're still together. . .even though we're not."

He nodded, leaning forward listening to what she said.

She sighed. "He doesn't make my heart race." She pointed to him. "It's like what you said about Kate. He doesn't make my heart race."

"But you've been with him for months," he probed.

She swallowed with difficulty. "Um, I do like that he's taller than me."

He sniggered. "That's very romantic of you to say."

Her body sagged with mortification into the plastic seat. "Mike didn't want me coming out on the date tonight, and we fought about it," she said, unwilling to meet his curious gaze.

"And yet you came," he said with a lazy lift of his eyebrow.

Yes, she had. It wasn't just about Rachel and her encouragement. It was also about her self-worth and taking a risk on happiness. She'd played it "safe" all her life. For once she wanted to do something that was so unlike her that she'd agreed to the date.

"Um, yes. I did think about it, and I decided it was a one-off opportunity I couldn't miss out on." That was the truth, and sounded better than her thoughts. "I mean, I don't think many Hollywood actors will be ringing me up to ask me to be their dates." She let out a laugh but even to her ears, it sounded forced and contrived. *I didn't want to miss this chance with you* was the real answer.

"I'm sure you'll work things out," he said with genuine acceptance.

She nodded. "Yeah, I mean, we're just old friends

catching up, right?" Her fingers fluttered to her throat.

A funny look crossed his eyes. "Yeah."

A pause hung between them as they gazed at each other. Her heart quickened, and she needed to fill the silence with chatter, pretend he wasn't affecting her like he was.

Because as handsome as he was, she was attracted to his kindness, his intellect, and his hard work ethic. Those qualities didn't disappear just because he was now a star.

"I'll speak to him this week, explain everything," she said. But they were just meaningless words. She'd started questioning herself, wondering why she was settling for someone who she didn't love. It was like what Sam had just said. Mike didn't make her heart race. If there was no spark, could one develop or was she whipping a dead horse?

The room became too small, too hot and too confining. She needed to get out, get some air. And create some space between them. As wonderful as Sam was, he'd never be interested in someone like her. She was an everyday gal, and he was a Hollywood star.

"Do you reckon we can go for a walk?" Her head nodded towards the beefy security guard standing there. "Will they allow it?" She really needed to walk and get out of the diner.

"I think so, we'll go towards the beach, the part where the boat launches are." He paused. "There shouldn't be too many people there at night."

"It's a cool autumn night and there aren't as many people walking along the foreshore as there are in summer," she said, hoping there wouldn't be anyone there, so they could escape the confines of the room.

"I've got hats and some bulky jackets in the limo... we can use those." He stood and held his hand out. "Let's go."

She looked around. "What about dinner? We need to pay?"

He chuckled with amusement. "I've already paid for it. Since we're their only customer tonight, I had to ensure they were compensated."

"Megan organised it?"

He nodded.

"Wish I had an awesome PA working for me."

They turned to the staff and waved. "Thanks, that was great," he said before they exited the café.

THE NIGHT AIR was cold and Sam was grateful for the jackets they wore and the baseball cap that shadowed his face. He liked that they looked like everyone else. Walking along the beach-side track, enjoying an evening stroll. He took a deep breath of the cold, salt-scented air and enjoyed a moment of thankfulness to be walking outside. . .alone.

"It feels good to be able to do this," he admitted to her, as they walked on the sidewalk. There was lighting, but it was dark and unlikely that the few passers-by would recognise him.

"You're famous. Unfortunately, you've had to give up some of your freedoms to be who you are," she said.

"That's very insightful and yes, you're right. In some parts of LA, I can get around because there are enough stars. But it's moments like this, I miss." He loved his career, and wanted it more than anything, and he'd accepted that being a star meant there were some things he couldn't do. He hadn't missed them much...until tonight.

One security guard walked a few metres in front, and the other stayed at a respectful distance behind them. But so far, no one had bothered them and he was enjoying this alone-time with Paige.

It was just the two of them, and he was enjoying his time with her. She didn't fawn over him like so many others did. He liked that.

He'd been surprised that she'd clammed up, talking about her boyfriend. He sounded like a tosser, and he was surprised that someone as smart and engaging as Paige would be with someone so...uninspiring.

She hadn't looked happy when talking about Mike, so he hadn't pressed her too much. He preferred when she smiled. It reminded him of those happy times so many years ago at school. Being with Paige was fun, and he was genuinely enjoying his time with her. Unfortunately, all too soon, the date would be over. Not only did he have to get up early for his trainer, but his day was chocked full. He needed sleep. But not yet.

"Tell me about your younger sisters? Is Poppy still as um, how should I say this? As flighty as she was in high school."

"Yep," she agreed. "She still loves dogs, and is wanting to make a career out of it. Since she left school, she works for six months and earns money, then travels. After she's run out of money, she comes back to Melbourne and starts again."

He chuckled. "That sounds like her. She didn't meet someone whilst travelling?"

"No, she prefers dogs." She laughed. "She needs a man who sees how kind she is and understands that she's pretty awesome even if she's not career focussed. Her dream job is looking after and being around dogs."

"And that man will have to be a dog lover?"

"For sure. Poppy's always finding stray dogs. She cares for them, cleans and feeds them, trains them and finds them forever homes."

"I always remember her as being kind," he said.

"Yep. As a teenager, she was seen as weird but that quirkiness as an adult is very endearing."

"And the other two?"

"You know about Phoebe, but Paisley is a nurse and also, now a single mum."

"Oh," he said, surprised about Paisley. "That's young. Did her husband die or something? I can't imagine her having an *oopsie* pregnancy…if you don't mind me saying."

She let out a long breath. "You're right. She's too sensible for that."

"And?" He asked wanting to know more.

The press of her lips said that she wasn't going to tell him much.

"Come on, I'm just asking as a friend. Who am I going to tell?"

She chuckled. "It's a long story. But she met the love of her life at university, fell pregnant and ah…is now a mum to a gorgeous boy."

"Where's the dad?" Now he was interested, and

not because he wanted to gossip but it irked him to hear that she was a single mother. Why wasn't the dad helping her out?

"He doesn't know." She raised her hands defensively, expecting him to ask more questions. "This is the way she wanted it. Something happened between the two of them, I don't know what. But ah, um, she thinks it's better this way."

He rubbed his chin. "The father has a right to know."

"I agree," she added. "Anyway, Mum helps her. She's delighted to have a grandson, after four girls. He's a sweetie."

"How old is he?"

"Lev is almost two years old."

He felt his forehead crease with surprise. Paisley had always been so sensible, and he was genuinely surprised that she was a single mum at such a young age.

"Tell me about you," he said, taking her hand as they strolled along.

Her gaze took in their hands, and a smile touched her lips. "Not as interesting as you but after school, I went to university. I intended to do Chemical Engineering as I love maths, physics, and chemistry."

"What do chemical engineers do?"

"Basically, you use science to turn raw materials

into something valuable or useful." She paused. "I loved the idea of designing processes that would convert chemicals into something we can use. But then my dad suggested doing Architectural Engineering instead."

"Isn't he an architect?" he asked, recalling how they often worked in his study, where a large table for drawing and designing dominated the room.

"You remembered," she said with joy in her voice. "Yes, he is. But what I chose to do focussed on designing and constructing buildings that don't harm the environment either during construction or during their lifetime."

"How long was your degree," he asked, curious about her career.

"I did an honours Bachelor of Engineering, specialising in Architectural Engineering, and it took four years," she said. "I got a great job working for a large company, and now I have a fancy title, *Structural Engineer*."

He could hear the pride in her voice.

"I knew you'd do well, you were so smart at school, always the top of the class with maths and the sciences," he said with genuine admiration. He'd always liked Paige. Despite her reserved nature and quiet disposition, she'd opened up with him. He remembered there were times they'd talk for hours.

Good times. Back then, she understood the pressure of being a teen star. Being famous from a young age came naturally to him, but he still craved his privacy.

"I guess I don't have to ask if you love your job," he said with a wink.

She gently punched his arm. "I love my job."

"Do you still skateboard?"

"What is it with you and all the questions? How do you remember all this stuff," she asked with a laugh.

"We're taking a trip down memory lane, I guess."

They shared a laugh as they both realised they were walking together. . .along a path.

"How did you stay so normal and nice?" she asked.

"What do you mean?" He wanted to know why she'd asked that.

"You're like a male diva. You have staff on hand, security," her head gestured to the men keeping a lookout for them. "Yet you seem so down to earth. I'm surprised, happily so, to see that you haven't become one of those stars who fire someone because their latte is not hot enough."

"That's just not me," he said. "My mum would probably clip me over the ear if I did that. You know that they relocated to LA to watch out for me."

"That mustn't have been easy."

"It wasn't. And after a few years, they moved back to Melbourne." He sighed reflecting on the day they left to return home. He'd smiled and said all the right things, but on the inside, it was like his internal organs had been shredded. He loved his parents and missed them a lot. Especially on holidays. There were times he wished he could pop over for a Sunday night dinner and TV movie with them.

"You must miss them, being so far away," she said breaking his thoughts.

"I do." He really did. "But they needed to come back to where their friends and family were." They'd hated the bustle of the large city. It wasn't for them. They'd moved to LA to help him settle into a new city when he was eighteen. But despite them trying, they'd never made many friends.

"When are you seeing them?"

"I already have, and then again after the tour."

His parents had never sold the family home, and he treasured the few times he was in Melbourne where they could be together, just like it had been when he was growing up.

He wanted to spend as much time as he could with his parents as he wasn't sure when he'd next come to Melbourne. His agent was eager to block his calendar with work for the next few years.

Paige stifled a yawn, and a quick check of his

watch surprised him at how much time had passed. They'd been talking for hours.

"As much I want to stay out here talking with you, I need sleep," he said with reluctance. His life was not his own. "I've got a session with my trainer in the morning and then back-to-back interviews for the next few days. I'm also flying to Sydney and all the other capital cities over the next week."

"You're a star, of course, you need to do what you need to do," she said slowly.

"You've always been the understanding one. I knew I wouldn't have to explain it all to you." Paige was never demanding or insincere. He'd really enjoyed tonight, shame he couldn't spend more time with her. But the trip to Melbourne was for work, not for socialising.

"I'm the smart sister," she announced, like it was a bad thing.

He scowled, not liking her being so dismissive of herself. "You say that like it's a bad thing."

She bit her lip and then shook her head. It looked like she was struggling with something she wanted to say. "Paige, are you okay?"

She nodded but didn't say anything.

"Paige?"

He saw her take a deep breath as though she needed it to steady herself for whatever she was about to say. It was unlike her. She'd always been so forthright and opinionated in what she said and thought.

"Tonight has been amazing, such a fun night that it all seems like it's a dream." She paused. "Thanks for letting me be your date. It was really special. I know it may not be for you, but it has been for me."

He started to interrupt her, reassure her that he'd also enjoyed the night, when she placed her finger across his lips.

She cleared her throat a couple of time. "Please let me finish, otherwise, I'm going to chicken out."

He nodded in reply, curious as to why she was so nervous. From the squeak of her voice, to the babble of her words tumbling from her lips.

"I know I shouldn't be doing this, but I really want to. Please excuse me, but I um, I just need to do this." She stood on her tip-toes so they were almost face to face. And then she kissed him... on the lips.

He gasped with shock, unable to believe she'd kissed him.

He pulled away. A knee-jerk reaction. He had not expected her to kiss him.

And despite the darkness, he could see her blanched face, self-loathing clouding her eyes. He could almost hear her berating herself at her actions.

"You surprised me," he murmured before his arm

looped around her waist. He tugged her, so she was flushed up against him. "Let's try that again." He didn't really think about it, because if he had, he wouldn't be kissing his friend. But it felt right, and so he leaned down and brushed his lips against hers.

He did it again.

And again.

And then his arms anchored her to him as he deepened the kiss.

He wasn't sure what to expect, but he welcomed her arms coming around his neck as she beckoned him to kiss her.

He couldn't explain it but their kiss felt so natural, so right.

He heard her sigh and his fingers trailed along the side of her face.

They kissed, and kissed, and kissed.

He deepened it further and she opened her mouth, welcoming his tongue. Their tongues duelled but it wasn't hot and heavy but reminiscent of his early teenage kisses. Eager. Playful. Connection.

Not once had he thought about kissing her, but now that they'd taken that step towards intimacy, he realised how much he liked it.

Shame he'd never get to see or kiss her again…in the near future.

His fingers trailed along the soft skin on her

cheek, and then along her jawline. As wonderful as their kiss was, he needed to say goodbye. Nothing could come of their kiss, and he certainly wasn't going to have a one-night stand with her.

She meant too much to him for that.

The coconut scent of her shampoo teased his nostrils as the cool salt air washed over them. He sighed and reluctantly ended the kiss. He stepped back and took in the flush of her cheeks, and the strong eye contact she maintained.

"You're a good kisser," she admitted with a smile.

"So are you." Damn good kisser, she was. He'd never expected to have enjoyed a kiss so much... from a friend.

"Did you mind?" She bit her lip, as though expecting him to disappoint her.

Placing his hands gently on her shoulders, he looked at her. "Being kissed by a beautiful woman? Most certainly not."

She rolled her eyes. "You know what I meant."

"It felt right," he said. And it had. They'd had this amazing time together, and their kiss had felt so natural. It hadn't felt weird at all. He brushed his lips against hers, needing to feel their softness one last time. "We need to go."

"I know." Her fingers rubbed across her brow. "It's all over."

He could hear the disappointment in her voice, and he felt it, too. But there was nothing he could do about it.

His life was crazy busy, especially on tour. He simply couldn't do what he wanted to do and disappoint his fans, or the media.

Taking her hand, they walked slowly to the limousine that was waiting nearby for them. They climbed in, sitting next to each other.

"Where do you live?" he asked, realising that despite their non-stop talking he didn't know where she lived…or if she lived alone.

"In Elwood," she said, mentioning a nearby suburb. "I've got this amazing art deco apartment, it's not that big but it's in walking distance to the beach and cafes."

"It's a pretty cool area to live in," he said.

"I love it there." He could hear the genuine pride in her voice.

"We'll drop you off before returning to the city," he said.

The drive to her apartment passed in a couple of minutes, thanks to the late hour and little traffic on the road.

In the darkness of the limo, they didn't talk much. He was used to a driver and security hearing everything he said, but was sure that it made Paige uncomfortable in the way she kept looking at them, and nibbling her lip.

The car stopped outside a brick apartment block that looked to house around six flats.

"This is where I live," she announced. "I know you need to sleep, but do you want to come in for a minute and see it. I'd love to show it off."

It was late, and he had a ton of messages on his cell that needed to be answered. He ran his fingers through his hair. Surely a few minutes wouldn't matter. "I'd like that," he said.

He opened the door, and holding hands, they made their way to her apartment.

CHAPTER 6

A few hours later, Paige heard a knock at the door. A look at her bedside clock told her it was six o'clock. She'd slept in, usually waking at five to go for a run before she got ready for work. The knocking persisted, and she walked to the door yawning.

"Who is it?" she asked through the door, rubbing her sleepy eyes.

"Sam! Open the door, *now*," he said in a stern voice.

Her heart quivered at the sound of his instruction. What was he doing here? She'd never expected to see him again, unless it was on a movie screen. Her heart sighed with a ridiculous amount of regret.

She swung open the door and he walked in, wearing sneakers, running shorts and a hoodie. He tugged the hoodie off his head and she gasped, seeing the tightness around his jaw and the deep lines on his forehead. His handsome face was marred with annoyance.

"I don't like being played. I thought we were friends." His dark eyes blazing with angst.

She shook her head and rubbed her eyes. "I don't know what you're talking about. I just woke up," she said before realising she was in her PJs, without underwear. "Sorry, I'll be back in a sec."

She ran to her bedroom and grabbed a robe which she drew around herself, tightly. "What's going on?" she asked, still groggy from being woken abruptly, as she walked back into her small lounge area.

Sam was standing, his spine ram-rod stiff, and an annoyed look still marred his face.

"You kissed me for a story. I can't believe you'd do that." He paused. "And by the way, here's your phone." He thrust her mobile at her.

She took it from him and saw countless missed calls from Mike, Rachel, and blocked numbers. Why was everyone calling her?

"You shouldn't use your birthday as your security code. I've checked all your messages, and deleted the photo of us I sent you," he fired at her, before he started to pace around the room.

"What? I don't understand. Why is everyone calling me? Who do you think you are reading my messages? How dare you." She felt like she was in the Twilight Zone, where everyone knew what was going on but she'd missed out because she'd been sleeping. What had happened in those few hours while she'd slept?

"How dare I?" he said walking right up to her. "Me? You kissed me, and it was all a setup. I can't believe I fell for it. And thanks to you and *your boyfriend*, I'm now going to have to deal with questions about me having sex with you…when you're engaged."

"What?" she gasped with outrage. "I didn't do any setup, Mike is not my boyfriend, and I'm not engaged."

"Mike, the guy whose heart is broken, says otherwise." He lifted his phone, pointing to it. He swore. "It would've been better if I could've come in here and slapped the newspapers down. More dramatic than pointing to an electronic device."

She resisted the urge to giggle at the drama. "I don't understand."

"I'm here to promote my new movie, not fend off questions about who I have sex with. The media loves it. And in case you didn't know, we had sex last night."

She scratched her head. "Really? I don't remember." *They'd had sex? Wow!* She wasn't sure whether she should jump for joy, or be disappointed that she couldn't remember it happening.

"No, we didn't have sex." He said in a tell-tale voice like she was a toddler. "But the newspapers have run with pictures of our kiss and us walking into *your* apartment. They didn't print any photos of me walking out ten minutes later."

"Oh," she said, the realisation of what was perceived sank in. Her legs felt as stable as wet mud, and she gratefully sank onto a nearby chair. "This is not good."

"No, it's not," he snapped, his eyes narrowing as he looked at her from across the room. "Plus, *your* idiot Mike is talking to anyone who'll listen."

"Mike? How did he get involved?" Her tummy rolled with concern.

"The media tracked him down and he's been talking non-stop. He seems to be enjoying his fifteen minutes of fame."

"I didn't speak to him last night," she said. After her amazing date and kiss with Sam, she went to sleep. "And I didn't have my phone," she added, even though that wasn't the reason she hadn't rung him.

"Well, the newspapers were tipped off, and the only people who knew where we'd gone were you and me. And since I didn't talk, it has to have been you." He said with determination and a nod of his head.

"What about your driver? The Security?"

He rolled his eyes. "You really don't understand my life. They work for me and have for years. I trust them." He paused. "I don't trust you."

"You've got to believe me, I didn't do any setup, I'd never do that to you," she said, desperate for him to know he'd made a mistake. How was she going to fix this?

"I don't believe you." He ran his hands through his hair. "I'd expect this from some desperate fan, but from you?" He looked at her with his dark eyes, filled with disappointment. "I thought you were my friend. It hurts that you've betrayed me. My team will manage the media. But to know that *you* did this...it stinks."

"But I—"

He lifted his hand, his palm facing her. "Stop. Just don't." He took a deep breath. "Apparently you entered my charity competition to win a date with me. We'll be removing all your entries, and the money you donated will be reimbursed to you. I don't want any chances of you winning a date with me."

"Sam, please let me explain," she said, desperate

to clear her name and let him know she didn't betray him.

"I went to so much trouble with the security last night to ensure we not only had fun together, but we got privacy. I did that *for you*. I didn't want our time together to be marred by the press." He stood straighter. "I'm hurt by what you've done."

Urgency pumped through her veins. She was desperate for him to know she didn't do it. "Sam, I didn't have my phone. I was with you the whole time. How could I have tipped off the press?"

He shook his head. "For someone so smart, I can't believe you wouldn't think of all the technology you could've used. A second phone? A tracking device? For goodness sake, you're embarrassing yourself."

Her lungs ached with remorse. It hurt so much that he thought she'd betrayed him to the media, something she would never do...and yet, it seemed she had. How else did the media know about her and Sam?

"You signed an NDA, my lawyers will recommend I sue," he said.

"Sue? Me?"

"You breached a contract," he said flippantly.

"I didn't do it," she said. "I promise you I didn't."

"I don't believe you. But because of our friendship, I'm not going to sue you. But I never want to see you again. Don't get in touch with me, and if you have any self-respect left, don't talk to the media."

"Sam, please." She stood and walked towards him. "There's been a mistake."

"There's no mistake. Goodbye Paige." And he spun around and walked out of her apartment, slamming the door behind him.

She sank onto the nearest chair, still quite unable to believe what had just happened. The most magical night of her life had turned into something sordid and distasteful. Their special kiss, something that was supposed to be just between the two of them, was now "news" in Australia. . .and perhaps in America, too?

She shuddered in revulsion and hurt. How had this happened?

She closed her eyes remembering every special detail of the previous night. They'd been alone, after the movie premiere, except for security. Had someone seen them at Leo's? On the beach? She rubbed her eyes with the balls of her hands. What a mess.

She lifted her mobile phone and looked at the number of missed calls. There were a lot, she noted, scrolling through.

And the message from Sam, with the selfie of them in the limo, was gone.

There was no evidence of their night together except what was in the press, and she didn't want to read *that*.

She dialled Rachel's number, and then stood and made her way to the kitchen. She needed a coffee.

HALF AN HOUR LATER, Paige opened the door and in strode her best friend carrying two large take-out lattes and a paper bag.

"Rach, you're the best," she said, closing the door behind her. "How did you get here so quickly?"

"I've been sleeping on the couch in these clothes, waiting for you to ring," her friend admitted.

Paige could see worry in the dark circles under her friend's eyes. "I'm so sorry that everything has gone pear shaped."

They sat opposite each other on the sofa and sipped their coffees.

"Tell me what happened?" Rachel's voice was filled with concern for her friend, and Paige was grateful to have her there.

Paige sighed before she recounted the day and night from the beginning, starting from when Lola and Jasmine dressed her to Sam bringing her home last night.

"Have you read the papers?" Rachel asked.

"No. And I don't think I want to," she confessed.

"It's probably a good idea," her friend admitted. "Why didn't you answer my calls and texts last night?"

"Sam's PA took my phone from me, and I only got it back this morning," she said with a despondent sigh. What's in the bag?" She pointed to it, sitting on the table.

"Your favourite, of course," her friend said with a cheeky wink.

"You're the best." She took the bag to the kitchen and lifted two almond croissants and placed each on a plate before returning to Rachel. "I feel like eating both, I'm so upset."

"Forget it," Rachel said, taking her croissant. She lifted her plate in the air as though toasting Paige. "Here's to us clearing up things between you and Sam."

"Thanks, but I have no idea how we're going to do it." Her heart ached over the pain of hurting Sam, and the frustration over how the details had been leaked to the media. She knew she hadn't done it. Had someone recognised them? But what about the security? The jackets and caps that obscured their features. Had someone noticed that it was Sam at the beach?

Rachel lowered her latte and looked directly at her. "I'm only asking this because I'm your best friend, but did you two have sex last night?" Her eyes gleamed with interest and she bit her lip in anticipation of what Paige was to reveal. It seemed she was hoping that they had.

I wish. "No," she admitted. "He came here last night, saw the apartment, and we chatted for a bit before he went back to his hotel and I went to sleep." She bit into her croissant, enjoying every flaky, delicious, calorie-loaded mouthful.

It was so unfair. Everyone thought they'd had sex...and they hadn't. How frustrating to be forced to defend herself. Like there was something wrong with her. She shook her head with disbelief at the ridiculousness of the scenario.

"Have you spoken to Mike?" Rachel asked, and she could hear the hesitation in her voice.

"No." She drained the last of her coffee, and placed the empty cup on the floor. "As I told you, I didn't have my phone with me." She sighed. "Rach, I made the decision to go out with Sam, even though Mike didn't want me to. It was a date with a friend. The problem for Mike is that he can't seem to accept that we're on a break. And that I asked for a break, *before* I knew about Sam."

Her friend nodded, not interrupting or passing judgement.

"Nothing happened."

Rachel's eyebrow lifted.

"Okay, so I kissed him, but that was it. And that was not planned, I just did it because I finally had the courage to do what I've been dreaming about for years. You know how much I *liked* him at school. It was a kiss. No groping or anything like that." She took a deep breath. "I can't believe Mike has gone to the media and told them we're engaged."

"Yes, that was news to me. I had no idea you two were getting married," Rachel said with a giggle. "I would've expected your best friend to know this."

"Last night was the best night of my life. I thought that everything would go back to how it was, AS, *After Sam.* But now everything is more muddled."

"But you kissed him," her friend interjected. "I don't usually kiss my friends."

"I didn't mean for that to happen, but I was caught up in the moment." She sighed with frustration. "But now that it has, it's another confirmation that Mike and I don't belong together. Because if we did, I wouldn't have kissed Sam."

Rachel waggled her finger. "You've had a crush on Sam since you were in high school, and you've built it up to a crescendo because he's a star in Hollywood. He's unattainable. Yet, you've created this fantasy about him. You don't really know him. You kissing him is part of that fantasy. It's not reality."

Paige scratched her chin. "I'm not following you."

"Sam is a fantasy. But he's a regular man who is like all men. If he wasn't a star and had a regular job, his habits of leaving his socks on the floor or not putting the lid back on the toothpaste would annoy you...like anyone. But you've made him into this perfect guy who can do no wrong."

Rachel lifted her hand to prevent Paige from interrupting her. "I'm your best friend, and have known you for years. You've thought about Sam, and put roadblocks between you and your boyfriends since Sam went to live in LA."

"You're making me sound like a nut case," she said, her tummy rolling with embarrassment, as shame washed over her.

"You're not. You've just had a crush...and it's grown over the past years. That's all. But Sam is guy, a nice one, and you've hurt him. You didn't mean to, but you did."

"I don't know what to do," she said, as she rubbed

the balls of her fists over her eyes.

"I'm sure Sam's PR team will work out something and they'll get you on board sometime today." She paused. "But it's time to move on from Sam."

"Have I been that bad?" she asked as mortification inched up and down her spine, listening to her friend speak.

"No, you haven't." She reached over and hugged her friend. "He's gorgeous, and it's perfectly normal for you to idolise him. You've had Sam on a pedestal, for years." She paused. "I know how many times you watched that video of him raising money for his charity."

Paige cringed with embarrassment. It was true. When Sam said, "Do you want to go on a date with me?" she pretended he really was talking to her. Pathetic. She really was pathetic. How had this crush grown to such an extent?

Gosh. She felt like a complete dunce and utter loser now. How had she got so caught up with Sam? If Rachel knew, what must her family think? She bit her lip, not wanting to even think about it.

"Was Mike my forever guy, that I blew off because of my crush on Sam?" she asked with defeat.

Rachel's forehead creased with concern for her friend. "I don't think so. Remember, you asked for a break before you knew about the date with Sam."

"You're right, but what a mess," she said. She ran her fingers through her hair, massaging her scalp.

"It will all work out." Rachel reached over and squeezed her hand reassuringly. She looked at her watch. "I have to go soon. I need to get to work. With the restructure, we've had to work extra hours. I was gutted that I couldn't be there for you yesterday."

"You're here now. Thank you. You're such a good friend." Paige gave her friend a warm smile. "You'll be getting some money back in your account soon. Sam is getting his team to refund my entries, so there is no chance of me winning the date."

Rachel's face fell. "I'm so sorry."

"It's okay. You need that money more than I. You're getting married."

Rachel's face lit up. "I know. I'm so lucky to have met Travis. Who would've believed you can find love at the office?"

"I'm so happy for you." And she was genuinely happy for her bestie who had fallen for her co-worker.

"Yep, Travis is perfect for me. You know I love that clean-cut look." Rachel chuckled. "Whoever said accountants are boring and not sexy has never seen some of the men who work in my company."

"Yep, I think I need to find myself a corporate

guy." Paige's lips twitched at her own joke.

"There's a good chance that Sam or his team are going to come by today so they can clear up this media mess. I think you should take a personal leave day," Rachel said.

Paige nodded. "That's a good idea. I can't see myself focussing on work today. Lucky it's not that busy at the moment, so my manager will understand."

"Keep me posted, okay?" Rachel stood and took her plate and empty cup to the kitchen. "I need to go, but call me if you need anything."

"You are the best friend, ever." Paige stood and gave her a warm hug. "And even though the date has been splashed across the media outlets, I want to thank you for trying so hard to give me what I dreamed of. A date with Sam. I had the best time with him." She paused. "I'm going to take your advice, and I'm going to let him go. You're right. He was my first crush, and my first love. It's time to move on." She blew out a long breath. "I promise you that once he's back in LA, and all of this topsy-turviness is behind us, I will start to date seriously, and never use *that clause* again in my relationships."

"You go, girl," Rachel said. "Now go and have a shower and get ready. I have a feeling you have a big day ahead of you."

CHAPTER 7

*P*aige was thankful she took her friend's advice to shower and change before she went online to read the papers and see what had been written about her.

No sooner was she in her favourite jeans, and T-shirt than there was a knock at her front door. She opened it, and in strode Megan wearing a sharp suit, and an intimidating look on her face.

"There is media outside. What the hell did you do? I told you to just smile and be an accessory to Sam. But no, you're just like all the other wannabes. Honestly Paige, I expected better of you."

Well, good morning to you, Paige thought. Despite the early hour, Megan looked sensational in her corporate outfit, making her feel like a child in her casual clothes.

"Thanks to you, we've been up all night fixing your mess." She strode in and sat at the small table Paige used for meals. Her paper files hit the table with a thump, and she continued as though she were in charge, and Paige had no input or say-so. Megan glared at her. "Can you come and sit here? I need to go through this with you."

Paige reluctantly sat opposite her, feeling like she was about to reprimanded by a school principal. She placed her hands in her lap and fiddled with the silver ring she always wore on her index finger.

"Thanks to you and *your boyfriend*, we've had to go into damage control." She paused. "I don't care what's happening between you and Sam. My job is to look after him, and his image." She rolled her eyes, as though she couldn't believe how stupid Paige was, and for a moment, she felt sorry for issues they were having to clean up.

Paige nodded. "Okay."

"This is how it is, the adults are in charge now." She cleared her throat before placing her hands, fingers interlocked on the table. "Sam is launching his latest movie, a rom-com, and we're going with an insta-love story with you and him."

"Us? Insta-love?" Paige could hear the desperation in her voice.

Megan continued, ignoring her interruption.

"We're in damage control and we're painting Mike as a desperate, jilted lover. Any unflattering photos you have of him will help. Our angle is that you and Sam have been corresponding over the years, and when you caught up in Melbourne it was love at first sight. This will fit in nicely with his image, and yours."

The way she said yours made Paige feel that this was not a compliment, and the uneasiness grew in her belly.

"You need to take some leave from work and spend all your time with Sam. We'll have pics with you dating, you'll need to follow his schedule when he visits the other capital cities for the film premiere. You need to be his accessory and. . .Do. As. I. Say."

"But Sam doesn't want to talk to me. That's not going to work." Her voice lifted and she could hear the desperation in her voice.

Megan rolled her eyes, as though she couldn't believe she had to deal with her, and Paige squirmed in her seat.

"Sam is an actor. He will act and pretend he has feelings for you. What happens away from the public eye is not his fans' concern. But you will be the adoring girlfriend while he's in Australia. You'll be doing interviews and some videos that we'll circulate on social media."

Paige felt her lip wobble and her belly roll. "I'm not an actor, I can't do it."

Megan swore under her breath. "You will be coached, seriously Paige." Megan rolled her eyes with exasperation. "You can keep your retro. . .70s look." Her finger swirled in the air pointing towards Paige, as she struggled to find the right words to describe her outfit. "But you need to look a lot better at the movie premieres." She pushed a note page towards her. "Write down your sizes and measurements, and we'll get some clothes for you. I can't have you wearing jeans and looking like *that*." She gave her outfit another look of disdain.

Paige was being steamrolled with decisive efficiency, no wonder Megan was Sam's PA. "Is Sam okay with all of this?"

"Of course. I work for Sam, and everything I do is in *his* interests," she snapped at her. "He trusts me, and you need to trust me, too."

"Okay, you obviously know what you're doing." She paused. "Sam's my friend, I didn't betray him, and I want to make this right."

"You all say the same thing...*it wasn't me*." She used a high-pitched voice when she said *it wasn't me*. "Sam is a highly paid, highly sought-after actor, and has a new movie starting soon. I'm not letting some...*friend*, jeopardise his career."

There were three knocks at the front door. Megan stood and pointed at her. "No, you stay here. Don't talk to anyone, and don't post anything on social media. You do? I'll be the one suing you." She gave Paige a warning glare, before she tossed her immaculate hair over her shoulder and stalked to the front door. There was a murmur of voices before a young woman strode in with two small suitcases.

"This is the stylist," Megan said, not even bothering to introduce them. It was obvious that Megan was in charge and in damage-control mode.

Paige decided to obediently accept whatever Megan said because Sam was her friend. Somehow it was her fault that he was in this mess. Everything could be acted out for the media. She'd get help and play the part of the loving girlfriend...till she was cut loose. She wondered what the reason would be for their break-up. So many thoughts zipped through her head. "I need to speak to my manager and organise my leave," she directed to Megan.

"After. But you do it where I can hear every word you say. From now on, I'll be watching *everything* you do." Megan sat on her couch, and started reading emails on her phone, thereby dismissing Paige.

The young woman, the stylist, gave Paige a weak smile before she started unpacking her products.

"You need to close all the blinds and curtains, so the media can't see in," she instructed.

Paige nodded obediently, did as she was asked and her tummy rolled, acknowledging this was going to be a long day.

Forty minutes later, Paige's hair had been styled and light makeup applied. A glance in the mirror had her smiling. The artist had done a good job, keeping her looking like herself and not overly made up.

"Thank you," she said. Conversation had been limited and stilted with Megan supervising everything that was being said.

Paige had had a chance to flick through the papers and had been shocked at the amount of detail that had been created of her and Sam's "relationship." Mike had effectively played the wounded "fiancé".

If there had been a chance of Paige wanting to reconcile with Mike, it was long gone now. There was no way she could be with someone who had betrayed her so. She'd ignored all his messages but did text him to say she'd call him later. She needed to break up with him properly, and ensure he knew there would never be any reconciliation. But she needed to do so when she had privacy.

He obviously still thought they were together, despite her asking for a break. She needed to end things in a way that he understood they would not be getting back together. She sipped some water but the turmoil rolling through her belly didn't dissipate.

"Pack your essentials. We're getting you some clothes, but you'll need some of your own," Megan said, barely lifting her eyes from her mobile phone. "You've got ten minutes."

In her bedroom, Paige stuffed her favourite T-shirts, jeans, underwear, and socks in a bag, with her toiletries.

Eleven minutes later, she asked Megan, "Can I bring my skateboard? Skating helps me relax?"

Megan expelled a long breath, like she was already fed up with dealing with Paige. "Fine, let's get going." She looked around the room. "There is a van outside for us, everyone is to get in and take your belongings. No one is to talk to the media. Ignore them. Let's go."

Paige exited her apartment last, after confirming all the lights were turned off, and the door securely locked. She couldn't believe the number of reporters on the sidewalk, all because of her moment of weakness when she kissed Sam. Flashes of light momentarily blinded her, and she trailed behind Megan clutching her bag and purse. She ignored the questions thrown at her, and within seconds, she was safely behind the tinted windows of the dark van which inched its way to the main road.

"We're going to the hotel in the city, via the secure back entrance so there shouldn't be any media." She instructed, like she'd been doing all morning.

"Paige, I've got a PR consultant who'll run through everything with you. Once she's happy with you, you'll do a couple of short videos together that we'll use on social media."

Paige felt nauseous. She wasn't an actor. And besides, Sam hated her, and had never wanted to see her again. And soon, they'd have to pretend to be lovers, smiling for the camera. "I can't do it."

Megan rolled her eyes. "I don't have time for this. Do some breathing or whatever. You brought this upon Sam, and you're going to clean it up." She paused. "When all of this is over, and Sam returns to home, I never want to see you say a word to the media. If you do, I will sue you and I will sue your friend, the one who contacted us."

"Keep Rachel out of this," she said, defending her best friend.

"Just do as we tell you, and everything will be fine," she said, not bothering to lift her gaze from her phone. "I've also put a tracker cn your cell so not only do I know where you are, I can see all your messages and everything you post."

"Is that really necessary?" Paige couldn't believe the level of privacy she was losing.

"Once we're back in the US and you are a distant memory, I will remove it. I will keep copies of anything that I believe to be incriminating."

"Isn't this illegal? What about my rights?"

"It's not illegal because you know about it. And you lost your rights when you sold out your story, breaching the conditions of your signed contract." Megan dismissed her with a wave of her hand.

Paige fell back against the leather softness of her seat and groaned softly. What a mess she'd got herself into.

THREE HOURS LATER, Paige felt tears burning her eyes. She was exhausted and frustrated. "I'm not an actor, I'm an engineer. Okay? I'm trying to do the best I can," she all but yelled at the PR coach. They were trying to help her but the relentless pushing in having her repeat the lines over and over again was tiresome.

"Let's take a break," Lara, the PR coach said in a soothing voice. "Ten minutes."

Paige ran to the bathroom and stood at the basin,

taking deep breathes. She had to do this. It was the only way she could right things for Sam. If only she could remember her lines and not cringe with embarrassment every time she looked at the camera. Did she have to remind them that she'd never done drama at school, preferring to excel in maths and sciences? She'd run a science lunch club for mis-fit students, like her, who were shy, lonely or both.

She didn't have the confidence to do what was required of her, and despite so many attempts, she looked awkward and cringe-worthy during the practice runs.

Outside, she made herself a strong coffee and nibbled a chocolate cookie. No one talked to her, and she felt as lonely as she had all those years ago, back at high school, during lunch breaks.

"You always liked coffee and chocolate together," a deep voice said.

Paige looked up, and her gaze met Sam's. Despite his handsomeness, there were tired lines around his eyes. "I thought you never wanted to talk to me again."

He took a deep breath. "I'm still hurt by what you did, but we need to fix this. My career and my reputation are too important to me to have the media speculating that I have affairs with almost-married women."

"There was no setup, and Mike's not my boyfriend or my fiancé," she re-iterated, but she may as well have not wasted her breath. He wasn't believing her, she could see it in the hurt across his dark eyes.

"We used to be friends, and that's what I'm focussing on. Let's just do what we need to do." He ran his fingers through his hair. "Has Megan gone through the schedule with you?"

She nodded. "I need to accompany you everywhere. Even if I'm not interviewed, she wants me there, looking adoringly at you."

"You can cut the sarcasm, but yes, you and me need to look like a team. Don't flinch if I hold your hand, accept any kisses on the cheek I give you, and act like we're best friends." He instructed, making her feel like she was stupid and not the super-smart nerd that she was.

"I keep trying to tell everyone that I'm not an actor. You know that. You know that I spent my lunch hours in the science labs. . ." She struggled to breathe as her lungs ached. "I'm trying to do the right thing. I want to make it right for you, but I'm not an actor. You know that, but everyone thinks that a PR coach is going to magically transform me into someone that I'm not."

Her impassioned plea softened the intensity in

his gaze. "I understand. How about I sit next to you when you do your lines, will that help?"

"Probably not, but thank you." She sipped her coffee and finished the cookie.

Lara motioned her back to the sofa, and Paige felt her stomach sink. Now she'd fumble her lines in front of Sam. This was getting worse and worse.

"Okay, let's take it slow," Lara reassured her. "Sam, why don't you sit next to Paige?" Her hand motioned for Sam to come forward.

He gave Lara an agreeable nod before he sat beside Paige, and took her trembling hand in his warm hand.

He must have seen the fear and stress in her eyes, because he leaned towards her and said, "Paige, you can do this." He looked at Lara and said, "Give us a minute, will you?"

Lara smiled and moved a few metres away, giving them some privacy.

Sam looked at her. "Remember at school…"

Paige slapped her hand over her eyes. "Don't remind me." Her heart sank as she recalled that time in English Lit when her bossy teacher, Mrs McFadden, had insisted that everyone in the class had to perform a piece from Shakespeare.

"You did it," he reminded her, still holding her hand.

"Only because you did it with me," she said in a dramatic voice. Her mind cast back all those years to when they'd performed a scene from *A Midsummer Night's Dream*. She'd played Titania who hears Bottom singing and wakes, then falls in love with him, thanks to the spell of the flower. Sam had played Bottom, and wearing a horse's head he'd found in the drama department, had spoken his lines perfectly. Whilst she'd read them from a piece of paper, the class had loved the frivolity and fun of the scene, giving them an enthusiastic applause at the end.

"You got an A+ whilst I got a B- since I was supposed to perform alone." She shook her head. "It never made sense why she marked it that way."

His finger came under her chin, and he tilted her face to look at him. "It doesn't matter. You were terrified, and you overcame your fears through acting. You did a really good job that day."

"Really? You're not just saying that?" Her breath hitched in her throat, curious to know what he thought.

He chuckled, and there was a gleam in his eyes. "No, I'm telling you, your acting was excellent. You read your lines without an error. The class loved your rendition of Tatiana falling for a man named Bottom with the head of a donkey."

Her shoulders slumped, and a smile touched her lips as she remembered the fun they'd had. Sam was right, the class had enjoyed their interactions, and the choice of scene had been a good one. She'd chosen it and had practiced her lines till she was virtually saying them in her sleep.

"I can do this?"

"You can do this," he confirmed, with a squeeze of his hands. "Come on, let's give it a try." He motioned to Lara, and soon enough the camera was videoing them.

For the next few minutes, she was able to say the rehearsed lines that flowed from her lips. Instead of looking at the camera, she often looked at Sam, smiling at him, the boy who was her friend back in high school. She forgot about his persona and his ability to command millions of dollars to star in movies. She simply focussed on the guy she knew who made her heart sigh with teen emotion thirteen years earlier.

"That was great, you two," Lara said. "We snapped some pics of you looking at each other, which we'll use on social media."

Paige felt all silly and warm on the inside. While Sam sat next to her, holding her hand, his thumb absently massaging her pulse point, she pretended things were as they had been the night before when it was just the two of them walking along the beach foreshore, when she mustered her courage and kissed him. Something she'd wanted to do for years and finally had the chance.

There wouldn't be any more kissing, but perhaps things could work out between them. They could be friends again, or at least he wouldn't think so badly of her someday.

She could only dream about that.

"Acting is what I do best," she heard Sam say to Lara, interrupting her thoughts.

Bang.

Paige's hopeful thoughts went up in flames and burnt to cinders. Their relationship couldn't be repaired, despite her assurances that she'd done nothing wrong. Pain needled into her heart. It was like losing Sam all over again, like when he left her to live in LA.

CHAPTER 8

Sam saw Paige's shoulders stiffen and her face whiten at the end of the taping. He wasn't sure what had upset her but the easy truce they'd formed had suddenly disappeared.

He excused himself to grab a coffee, not really wanting one, but needing some time to himself. His bedroom afforded him the most amount of privacy of the suite. No one barged in, and rarely did anyone vie for his attention in here.

He left the unwanted cup on a nearby table, and he stretched out on the bed, not even bothering to remove his shoes. He was tired, jet-lagged and irritable.

The excitement of being with Paige, after all these years, had been obliterated by their kiss being plastered on social media. It was unlike Paige to do something as conniving as the setup, and he was surprised that so much evidence pointed towards her. Now that he'd calmed down, doubt had niggled into his belly, making him wonder if Paige was behind the scandal or someone else.

The Paige he knew was kind, caring, and quiet. Even last night, she had the same qualities that she'd had when he knew her back at school. She shunned controversy or being in the spotlight. Being surrounded by her friends and family was what made her happy, not being on the covers of magazines and newspapers.

But his team in LA had insisted that it had to be Paige. But they didn't know her like he did.

He was determined to find the perpetrator who had leaked the details to the media, and his security details were looking into it. Hopefully, they'd have an answer soon.

In the meantime, the controversy meant he and Paige would be spending time together, and surprisingly, he was looking forward to it.

Closing his eyes, he did some deep breathing to relax his muscles and his mind. And within minutes, he'd fallen asleep.

A KNOCK on the door jarred him awake, and a look

at his watch told him he'd been asleep for half an hour. "Come in."

The ever-efficient Megan walked in. Despite the lack of sleep, she looked flawless. She really was the best assistant he could ever ask for,

"Sorry to wake you, but you have a busy afternoon," she said. "You've got interviews with the media. They're waiting in the lounge area. I'll set you up and they can come in, one at a time. They know they've got five minutes each, and no questions about Paige."

He sat up and raked his fingers through his hair. "I need time to change."

"Sure," she said. "And then we'll head downstairs for your session."

"We're doing it here?" He rubbed his chin. His team had organised for him to meet underprivileged students who wanted to be actors. This was his passion...helping those who couldn't afford classes and providing them with scholarships.

"After the security breach last night, we're running the event in the ballroom here at the hotel," she instructed.

"Remind me to double your bonus this year. I don't know how you do it, but you are one helluva assistant and organiser."

His compliment made her tough look falter, and

she gave him a smile. It didn't often happen. Megan had little social life, and her days were devoted to him. But she was paid handsomely for being on call 24/7.

"You've got fifteen minutes to freshen up, I'll see you outside," she said before stalking out the door.

TWO HOURS LATER, Sam was glad to be finished with the interviews. Everyone had asked the same questions, and there were moments when he could feel his smile slip, and boredom worm into his replies. He'd started acting, because that was what he did best. As much as he loved promoting his movie, he couldn't wait to meet the students.

The media had left when Paige was ushered in.

"How's your afternoon been?" he asked, curious to know how she'd spent the past few hours.

"Okay," she said.

He could tell she'd been bored, not just from the tone in her voice, but also the sparkle in her eyes was missing.

Her chin lowered to her chest. "I've been provided with some clothes, so I look good next to you." She made quotation marks in the air when she said, "look good".

"It's only for ten days," he said, trying to lift her spirits.

"I know, but I can't help feeling out of control. Everyone is busy doing something except me," she admitted.

She wasn't used to his life, and he had to remind himself that she needed time to adjust to being in the media limelight. "My team is efficient, they're there to help you." He paused. "We have a number of events to attend, so you'll need the extra clothes."

She nodded in reply, but her eyes were vacant. "I know. I don't want to let you down, or impact your image by wearing something inappropriate or wear the same outfit twice."

"Trust Megan and the stylist, they know what they're doing."

She nodded again, but this time he could see the pallor of her face wasn't as noticeable as it had been seconds ago.

He reached for her hand. "Come downstairs with me." It wasn't a question. He wanted her there, wanted her to see an area he was passionate about. This is where he wanted to make a difference and help those less fortunate than his teen-self.

She raised her eyebrows, obviously curious. "Where to?"

"I'll tell you on the way," he said with confidence.

"Come on, you'll enjoy this more than waiting for me in the suite."

* * *

PAIGE, feeling comfortably dressed in her own clothes, stood back and watched the event with interest. The room was filled with about one hundred teenagers, and their focus was on Sam. They'd been invited to meet him, and he was currently inspiring them with a speech about his journey from Melbourne to LA.

She gasped when Sam told the audience about *her*. Her. Everyone turned their head to look at her, and she squirmed in her sneakers.

Sam continued. "Paige was a good friend at school. She was always there when I needed help. I missed many days of classes going for auditions. She coached and helped me when I was behind." He paused. "Be like Paige. Help each other out. Be there for each other. You need to finish school. And you need an education. And if you have a friend like Paige, let them know how much they mean to you. Because without her, I wouldn't have finished school."

Paige's heart pounded so hard against her chest that the rhythm blocked out the rest of Sam's speech.

She couldn't believe he'd said that. . .publicly. Had he meant it or was he just being kind because she was now his fake girlfriend?

She wanted to believe he genuinely liked her, but after the debacle over their kiss, she wasn't sure.

At the conclusion of Sam's speech, the students stood giving him a standing ovation. They were then provided with a questionnaire and had thirty minutes to complete it.

"What are they doing?" she asked Megan, curious to know more. Megan still terrified her, but she preferred to direct her questions to her. Besides, as his "girlfriend," Paige should've known more about this.

Megan's face softened. "The students will give us a rundown of their experience and reasons for being an actor. We'll invite the top twenty back and get them to do an audition for us."

"And then what?" She leaned forward to hear more.

Megan checked the time on her mobile phone before continuing. "Some will be chosen to be recipients of a scholarship. Sam will pay for their tuition to attend any one of Australia's top acting schools."

"Wow," she said. "That's so generous of him." A buoyant feeling of inspiration warmed her belly.

"Don't repeat it." Megan's chin lifted. "Sam doesn't want this being leaked out."

"I promise," she replied with sincerity. She had no intention of letting Sam down, and also the students. This was an amazing opportunity for some of the teens here. "I really like how Sam is giving back, helping with his time and money."

Megan gave her a stiff nod in acknowledgement, as though she couldn't believe Paige would think otherwise of Sam.

"We're flying to Sydney tonight, and tomorrow will be the same. Media interviews, teen meet/greet and then attending the movie premiere," Megan said in her usual clipped voice.

"That's a hectic schedule." A brittle laugh came out of her lips. Not only was she nervous, but she was totally intimidated by Megan, Sam and being the girlfriend to a celebrity.

Megan shrugged, seemingly unphased by the schedule and Paige's nerves. "The following day we head to Brisbane, then we do Adelaide, Hobart and then back to Melbourne."

Paige felt her forehead crease. "We're not going to the other state capital cities?"

"No, there's not enough time. After his date, the one from his charity competition," she clarified. "We return to LA, and Sam gets ready for his next movie."

"Is it a rom-com?" she asked, curious to know if he was going to do another fun movie, or return to a more serious acting career.

"Yes," she said. "It's a romantic lead, so we need his public love life to reflect who he is. His image is important to him, and his career." She gave Paige a death-stare. "Just do what you're told, and everything will be fine. As I said, the adults are in charge now and I expect you to follow my direction."

Paige stared at Megan, wondering what it would be like to be her? Did she have a secret fantasy of being with Sam? Or did she have a boyfriend?

"Your thoughts are so noisy," Megan said with a toss of her hair. "And no, I'm not interested in Sam *like that.*" She turned on her heels and sashayed away from her.

Soon enough, the event was over, and the students filed out eager to retrieve their mobile phones which had been "confiscated." It had been part of the security plan.

Her mobile phone vibrated in her pocket. She checked the message. "Get organised. You have ten minutes upstairs before we head to the airport."

She looked up. Megan was standing a few metres away from her. Their gazes clashed.

"Hurry up," Megan snapped at her, and Paige saluted her, before heading towards the elevators.

. . .

A PRIVATE JET had been organised for Sam and his team, and Paige was suitably impressed at the five-star treatment she was enjoying. Out of the public eye, there was no need for Paige to be next to Sam, so she was relegated to the back seat while Megan and others chatted with Sam about his itinerary and security.

Paige was exhausted, and closed her eyes, willing herself to sleep, but she couldn't. Her mind was active, and she couldn't slow the thumping of her heart, despite all the deep breathing she was doing. She was on an adventure, the first in her lifetime and excitement bubbled through her veins.

In Sydney, they were whisked to the five-star hotel in a stretch limo, and soon they were seated in a cocktail bar. The area where they were had been roped off so there was no intrusion, but onlookers could see them. And some were taking photos, using their mobile phones.

"I feel like a monkey in a sideshow," she confessed. She sipped her drink, unsure what she should be doing. "I'm not used to such attention."

He nodded in reply. "We need to be seen out together," he reminded her, seemingly unfazed by the attention. "It's to fix everything."

She sighed, feeling responsible yet again for the mess she'd unwittingly created. "I know, but it feels weird. You seem to take it in your stride. You're just not bothered with fans over there taking photos of us."

"It's part of the job. Normally I'd be signing autographs and posing for photos, but Megan felt we needed some alone time."

"That's, um, ah, nice of her...I think," she said.

"I agreed with her, but I didn't want you to be barraged by fans. Most are very respectful but sometimes there are incidents where someone is rude, and I didn't want a fan upsetting you."

Gratitude whooshed from her lungs, and she sank into her chair. "Thank you, that's very considerate." Insecurity ate into her belly, reflecting on how different Sam's life was to hers, and she didn't like his much.

"You'll need to pretend you're enjoying being with me," he said. "You're looking too serious."

She flashed him a wide smile. "Better?"

"Perhaps." He stood, leaned across the table and brushed his lips against hers. "That's better."

Her body went from hot to cold, then hot again. The feel of his soft lips against hers made her tummy do cartwheels. One of the sexiest guys on the planet had just kissed her, and even if it was for show, it felt amazing.

Her fingers touched her lips, and she stared at Sam.

Unlike her, he seemed unaffected by their brief kiss as he sat opposite her, toasted her with his glass of red wine before drinking slowly.

This was Sam, the guy she'd had a crush on for so long, she didn't remember a time that she didn't. And now they were having "alone-time", and he'd kissed her. It may have been for show, but she didn't care. She loved it.

Her dreamy thoughts were interrupted as the man who'd introduced himself as the manager appeared at their table with some appetisers for them. "Steamed dumplings and mini-meatballs. Enjoy," he said with a flourish of his hand.

"Thank you," she replied, before returning her attention to Sam. "This smells delicious. I'm so hungry."

He lifted his eyebrow with concern. "You didn't eat on the plane?"

"To be honest, I was too nervous and excited. I just couldn't." She took one of the sticks and ate the meatball. "It's delicious."

The alcohol in the fruity cocktail she'd ordered relaxed her, so now she was smiling because she wanted to, not because she had to. After some chit-chat as they ate the food, she said, "What you said about me today in front of the teens was really nice."

"I meant every word." He leaned over and placed his hand over hers. "I missed so many lessons back in high school. I was lucky and ended up in Hollywood with a contract, not everyone gets such a break."

"That's why you encouraged everyone to finish school, complete their education," she asked, wanting to know more.

"Yes. The movie industry and also theatre is hard to break into. So many talented actors miss out, and only a few become stars." He paused. "It's important to have an education."

"I like that you're giving back," she admitted. "Those students are really lucky to hear you speak and learn from your experience."

He shrugged off her compliment, but he did reward her with a dazzling smile. "I was fortunate my parents could afford acting classes, but not everyone can."

She ate two more dumplings, which were not only perfectly cooked but absolutely delicious. "Does the questionnaire help you choose who is more deserving?"

The skin between his eyes crinkled. "Everyone is

deserving, but the questionnaire helps us see who is really *hungry* to be an actor. It will help us see who has the drive, determination and will to stick to it."

"How many will get scholarships?" she asked, her head tilting to the side.

"I don't know. It could be all of them, or it could be none of them?" His chin lifted and his chest seemed to puff out with pride.

"Really?" She blinked rapidly, wondering if she'd heard correctly. *All* of them? That was a lot of students to support.

"Yes. I don't put a number on the successful applicants we accept. We want the best, and determine that by reading their applications. Once we've sorted through them, we invite a number of students to act in a five-minute performance. They have time to prepare for the audition, it's not blind."

"That's enough time to see who is the best candidate?" Her voice was filled with wonder as she leaned closer to him, eager to hear more.

"Yes, they stand out from the others," he said. "You can tell once they're up on stage who'll be making it through."

"But they're nervous?" Her skin warmed, thinking back to high school when she had to perform in front of her class.

"Most are, they are teenagers. However, the talent shines when they're in character. I just see it."

"You do all the choosing?"

He chuckled. "Well, it is my money."

She grinned in return. "I think it's very admirable."

His brow lifted in reply and she could see the way his face had softened that he liked her compliment.

He drained his wine. "Did you have any problems getting leave from work?"

She groaned thinking about the phone call with her manager. She'd had him on speaker, so Megan could listen in. She's been so nervous that she'd stumbled over her words and her manager was not happy. It wasn't really a request, she'd "told" them she needed the time off.

"I hope I have a job to go back to next week," she said softly. They were in the midst of a large project, and she was needed at work, not flying around the country with a movie star. Her manager had referred to her as unprofessional and inconsiderate, and she was deeply worried about losing her job.

She'd also sent a couple of texts to Mike, explaining as best as she could. Megan had checked them, before sending them, of course.

It felt wrong having Megan read/listen in to her private conversations. Especially with Mike.

"Thank you for being here, and doing everything Megan has asked of you," he said interrupting her thoughts.

"I want to make this right. I know you don't believe me, but I didn't do anything to compromise you. I'm here now to fix things for you." She pressed her lips together in determination. Until security worked out the breach, she was the culprit. She hated that. But for now, she was going to do everything right by Sam.

"Thank you," he said, with genuine appreciation.

She squirmed in her seat as his dark eyes blazed at her, as though he could see all the way down to her soul.

"We have a busy day tomorrow," she said, changing the subject, diverting attention from the fluster she was feeling.

"I'll be up early as I need to exercise," he added, with a wave in the air.

She felt herself blush, like a sixteen-year-old, thinking of his abs and physique. She really needed to get over her crush. She was almost thirty. "Would you mind if I join you? I usually jog each morning along the beach." She really needed to exercise to clear her head, and besides, she'd have a good excuse to check him out while he did, too. Again, she knew she was pathetic. The crush was there. She couldn't pretend it wasn't, snap her fingers and make it go away. So for now, she'd enjoy each naughty, stolen moment she could.

"My trainer works me hard, so I'll be happy for the company. I'll meet you in the gym at 5 am. Don't be late."

"I'll be there." Of course she would. Any chance to see him sweat and lift weights.

Yep, pathetic. She mentally high fived herself in recognition.

THE FOLLOWING day passed in a blur of busy-ness. She and Sam were together a lot, but never alone. There was always someone around, whether it be Megan, security, or simply. . .someone. There was no privacy, and Paige was decidedly uncomfortable. Sam, she noticed, took it all in his stride, and was outwardly, genuinely friendly with everyone. He never seemed to mind the constant interruptions, or that he was never by himself. His smile was real, and she liked how he treated his staff with kindness and respect.

His PR team had organised meet/greets all over Sydney, and they spent much time in luxury minivans being whisked around the city. That night was another movie premiere and almost identical to the Melbourne one.

She and Sam held hands walking down the red carpet. She smiled as he chatted with fans, but kept a respectable distance from him during selfies but was back by his side when chatting with the media.

And like in Melbourne, they left via a back entrance, not staying to watch the movie.

Alone in the limo, except for security and the driver, she asked, "Are we going back to the hotel?"

"No, I have a surprise for you," he said, and she could hear excitement in his voice.

Something for her? She wanted to know more. "Tell me," she asked, not bothering to hide the eagerness in her voice.

He lifted his brow and chuckled. "Patience m'dear."

Fifteen minutes later, the limo stopped and he helped her out of the car. The area was deserted, yet the air was filled with the noise of commuters crossing the Sydney Harbour Bridge.

Her forehead crinkled, unsure of where they were. The darkened windows had made it difficult for her to see where they were.

Sam's voice interrupted her thoughts. "I organised this for you. It's not only a thank you for being my fake girlfriend, but also for being there at school…when I really needed you. We're at the—"

"Planetarium." She gasped with delight. Her head turned from side to side. "There doesn't seem to be anyone else around."

"No, it's just us." They started to walk to the building. "Part of the surprise is you meeting Professor James Burns." He named off one of Australia's best scientists.

"Ohmygawd, I admire his work so much," she gushed. Professor Burns. She was meeting Professor Burns. Her heart picked up a notch, with excitement.

"To be honest," he said with a shy voice, "I have no idea what an astrophysicist does."

She filled him in. "They seek to understand the universe and our place in it," she explained. "What's interesting about astrophysics is that it uses physics to understand astronomy."

He nodded in reply but didn't say anything.

"Professor Burns' latest paper on the origin of mass in the universe following the Big Bang was so interesting. I can't wait to ask him questions about these new insights," she admitted, sounding like a total geek, but not really caring. She was about to meet Professor Burns.

"Then we're having supper," he informed her.

Her smile widened, if that was at all possible. "Outside? Here? Under the stars?"

"Yes," he said with a nod.

Excitement and joy burst inside her at the unique gift he'd planned for her. Unable to restrain herself, she threw her arms around Sam's neck and kissed his cheek. "Thank you, that is the best present *ever*." She tugged at his hand, "Let's go."

THE NEXT HOUR passed very slowly for Sam. In fact, he'd checked his watch so many times in the past three minutes that he started scrolling through his social media accounts. Paige, on the other hand, exuberantly chatted non-stop with the staff and scientist.

It pleased him to see her energy, effervescence, and exhilaration. Most of his dates liked luxury clothing, jewellery, and fine dining. Paige was not like that, and he was impressed with himself for finding a gift that made her so happy.

The conversation revolved around stellar dynamics, galaxy formation, and evolution, astroparticle physics and other topics that he'd never heard of. He struggled to focus on what they were discussing, and soon the conversation turned into white noise where he felt like he was the class dunce.

He'd barely passed his high school exams in science, so this branch of space science where they were chatting about the laws of physics and chemistry to explain stars, planets and other objects in the universe made no sense to him.

He politely excused himself and no one really noticed as he made a hasty exit to the outside.

A table had been laid out for them by his staff and he sat on one of the seats ready to scroll through his social media. But he wasn't interested. For the first time in a long time, he was alone. He took some long, deep breaths and stared out at the view, taking in the lit-up Sydney Harbour Bridge against the glittering backdrop of North Sydney and Luna Park, a carnival theme park.

He left his mobile phone on the table, face down and just watched the cars driving across the Bridge in this tiny oasis in the middle of the city.

His security team was around, but he couldn't see them. He savoured this time alone, something that happened so rarely.

His thoughts drifted to his new movie, and the one he'd be starring in soon. Being a lead in a rom-com was exciting and mostly fun. He'd enjoyed his last movie and couldn't wait to start the next.

Branching into different acting paths was important to him and he was determined to maintain his place with Hollywood's best before he was knocked off by some up-and-coming hotshot. It would come, and some actor would eventually take his place. Just like he'd done to some other "ageing" actor.

At thirty, he was getting "old," so being able to work on rom-coms had been a smart career move. And he was glad he enjoyed it so much.

Paige interrupted his thoughts. "It's so beautiful out here," she sat opposite him at the table. "I'm sorry for talking for so long. But what a rush to talk to Professor Burns. I admire his work, and it was such a pleasure to meet him. Did you know he's got a job working for NASA? He leaves for America soon." She fanned herself using her hand. "I've had a total fan-girl moment. Thank you."

"You're welcome," he said.

A staff member approached him. "May I serve supper?"

"Thank you," he said. And the next few minutes involved a range of mezze plates being added to the table, and wine being served.

"Cheers," she said, lifting her glass to clink his. "Thank you for this picnic. It's the nicest one I've been on, with these beautiful plates and fine glasses. And even pretty tea lights."

She tried everything, from the mini-arancini balls to the sliders. Most of his dates rarely ate. They were in the public eye, and couldn't afford to put on any weight.

"I know it wasn't you who tipped off the media about us," he said in a low voice.

"I told you," she said, letting all her frustrations out in three simple words. She paused. "You should've believed me." She lowered her silver cutlery to glare at him.

He blew out a frustrated breath. "Give me a break. I deal with this type of stuff all the time." He paused. "I was also tired, jet-lagged and cranky after Megan had vented at me for what seemed like a day."

"Fair call. I get it," she said, as a sympathetic look crossed her eyes. "So what happened?"

"One of the staff at Leo's rang a TV network. He thought he'd make money out of it." He rolled his eyes at the stupidity of the staff. He'd compromised their security but had earned no reward.

"I hadn't thought about that. There were a couple of guys in the kitchen, and they must have recognised you."

"That, and the fact that I'd booked Leo's out for the night," he admitted with a chuckle.

"That too," she grinned in reply. "And don't forget the security guard at the front door."

Their gazes met and they chuckled. Yep. The bleeding obvious.

"I'm glad it wasn't you," he confessed in a low voice. And he was. It'd been a relief to confirm what his gut had known. Paige was true and honest. "But what about your ex? He seemed genuinely upset about us being *together*."

A funny look crossed her face before she bit her lip, as though she was searching the right words to say. "I've reminded him, yet again, that we're not together. And after how all of this has played out, I'd never date him again."

She was obviously uncomfortable about the situation, and he wasn't going to push her now. He was enjoying himself, and feeling relaxed, much better than sniping at each other.

Tonight was all about him and Paige. He sipped his wine. "Paige, if you didn't set up the media, why did you kiss me?"

She stopped eating, her cutlery dropped to the tablecloth and her jaw dropped, giving her mouth an O appearance. Her eyes widened but she said nothing.

CHAPTER 9

*P*aige felt ill. She'd had this amazing experience with Sam, and now he knew she wasn't the culprit. But now she had to deal with the kiss. Bugger. She didn't know what to say. She turned her gaze to her lap and fiddled with the creamy white cotton napkin.

"Paige?" His voice was insistent, wanting answers.

She wasn't an actor, and could never come up with a story when needed. It always came to her at a later date. If she told him the full truth, she'd come across as a desperate loser. She'd just try and spin it so she didn't look too hopeless.

She rearranged her cutlery, took a sip of wine and cleared her voice. "We may have known each other at school, but I haven't seen you for years.

You're now an actor that is known worldwide. You've become *someone* whilst, I'm still me, with my degree and three sisters."

"And?"

"Well, um, I guess I got caught up in the excitement of the night. I mean, I went as your date to a movie premiere where people were screaming your name. But then you booked out a café, so we could have dinner alone and then we walked along the St Kilda foreshore. It was a dream date, and at the time...it just felt right. And, um, you've always been special to me. And I may have *liked* you, as in *liked* you, at school." The words tumbled from her lips. She lifted her gaze and met his. There was warmth there, and his lips had curled into a small smile.

"I may have known that you *liked* me, at school," he admitted slowly. "But that feels like a lifetime ago."

Her skin burned with embarrassment, and she gulped some water down.

"But I felt like you, on our date. I don't normally kiss friends. Perhaps it was the rush of emotions from being together after so much time apart?" His voice was thick with emotion.

"Perhaps?" She said demurely as her tummy rolled with surprise. He felt the same? Wowsers! "It was really good to catch up, not just chatting but also going at Leo's."

"So which date is your favourite?" he asked, wanting to know more as he clasped his hands together.

She stifled a giggle. The one where they kissed would always be her favourite but she wasn't telling him that. Instead, she said, "Tonight. Because it was a really thoughtful date bringing me here. I mean, I don't know how you got the professor here on such short notice, but meeting him was definitely a highlight."

"You can thank the ever-efficient Megan," he drawled.

"Is there anything she can't do?" A rush of air left her lungs. "Does she ever sleep?"

Leaning back in his chair, he looked towards the Bridge and said, "She's a brilliant assistant. I couldn't do what I do without her."

"Does she have a life? Apart from looking after you, I mean?" She was so devoted to Sam, and Paige was curious if Megan had time to date or be with someone special. Unlikely, but she was still curious.

"Not really." He stroked his chin. "When she started working for me, she knew she'd be on call 24/7. Her career is important to her," he said in a matter-of-fact voice. "And I am thankful for it. I don't have time to do the things she does. She's efficient and dependable."

"If you fell for her, it could be like a Hollywood romance movie." She raised her eyebrows in reply. Not that she wanted Sam to fall for Megan, it was just a thought.

"I don't think so." He shook his head.

"Because she doesn't make your heart race?" She suggested.

"Yes, but also, I don't date the staff. It's in their contracts. I never want the people I work with to think I'm hitting on them."

"That makes sense," she said. She privately liked that he wasn't interested in Megan, even though that made no sense to her at all.

"I have to ask, is there anything that the media can use against you? I'm sorry to ask, but as my *girlfriend*, they may look into you, especially as we're going with this insta-love relationship."

She shook her head, her mind skipping over the past few years with rapid consideration. "No. I went to university, studied and started working. I haven't travelled much, and I spend way too much time with my family."

"I know, you love them a lot. You've always been close." He sipped his wine, his focus on her.

"The media may wonder why we're together."

Wasn't that the truth? "I mean, you usually date models and actresses." The reality of their situation weighed heavily on her shoulders. His team may promote their insta-love, but would his fans, and the media really accept and believe it? Look at him, look at her.

"It's not easy meeting women," he confessed. He fiddled with his water tumbler, reflecting on his words.

"Really?" She felt her forehead crinkle at the ridiculousness of his comment. It seemed so unlikely. I mean, this was Sam, gorgeous, talented, rich. He must have women pushing each other aside to get to him.

"No, really. I'm surrounded by people but they're all in the industry. It's not like I can just go to a bar and start chatting with women, getting to know someone." He had a distant look in his eyes that made her think that he was being honest with her, and not creating some whimsical story for her attention.

She watched him for a moment. He was right. He couldn't go out in public and be like everyone else. "Do you wonder if people like you for who you are? As in the person inside you, rather than Sam the star?"

His lips twitched with amusement. "Of course, all

the time. That's what I meant before. I'm well known so it's really hard to meet someone who doesn't think they know me." He paused. "I would like to meet someone, but I've got movies to make."

"You don't want to get married?" Her breath hitched in her throat as she waited for him to answer.

He stretched his legs out, as he leaned back into his chair. A small smile touched his lips. "Yes and no. My parents are happily married, and most of my family are, too. But I'm in Hollywood and surrounded by broken marriages, cheating and a whole lot of other stuff."

"It doesn't sound very nice." Her nose crinkled with distaste.

"It's not all bad, but it's not everyday life. It's different." He sipped his wine. "Being with someone in the industry could be good because she'd understand the demands on me."

She nodded. "That makes sense. But if you're with an actor, and she has to be on set away from you—"

"That's an issue. It's one of the reasons, I haven't dated someone long term." He blew out a long breath, as though he wished things were different.

Curiosity made her ask. "But what if you found *the one*?"

"The one? As in *the one*?" he said theatrically.

"Yes, if you found the one, and she was an actor and you had conflicting timetables with movies. What would you do? Hypothetically speaking, of course."

He gave her a tilt of his head in acknowledgement. "Of course, hypothetically speaking." He ran his fingers through his hair, before he leaned forward his arms resting on the table between them. "I don't know. We both need to work. One of us has to give up something for the other, otherwise, we'd be apart." He paused. "That's an issue when two stars are together."

"Yes." What he said made sense. Movies took time to film and produce, and it wouldn't be easy being married to someone with clashing work commitments. She shuddered, wondering how couples managed to stay together when spending months apart. Did it lead to infidelity?

"I want to marry one day, and can only hope that she can work in with my life." He pressed his lips together as he reflected. "My work is demanding on me, and those who are close to me."

"That's selfish of you. . .that she works in with you." She gave him a cheeky wink so he knew she was having fun at his expense.

He lifted his brow and his gaze clashed with hers,

"What can I say? I'm a superstar and a diva." He pretended to flick hair over his shoulder.

Their shared laughter made her insides warm with wistful longing. She couldn't imagine him being difficult and rude to anyone. She'd seen him with his staff and also the hotel staff. He was courteous and respectful...qualities that he'd had when he was younger, and hadn't left just because he was an actor who could demand millions for each movie he starred in.

They finished their meal, and Paige leaned back into her chair as she sipped her herbal tea.

As relaxed as she was, and as happy as she was in Sam's company, a niggle prevented her from being totally at ease. Her celebrity pass condition.

She clenched her teeth, as she considered whether to tell Sam or not.

He needed to know if there was something from her past that the media would love. She'd had few boyfriends, and at Uni had studied hard, rarely attending parties. The media would think she was "beige" however, would any past boyfriends say something about her stipulation about Sam? Was that juicy enough that the media would be interested?

She couldn't imagine so, but she'd rather eat a

live cockroach than tell this to Sam. It was embarrassing.

Best to speak to Megan, and let her manage it.
She'd rather Megan laugh at her than Sam.

But for now, it would be her secret. She just
needed to find the right time, away from prying ears
when she could confess everything to Megan.

"It's getting late," he said, interrupting her
thoughts. "We should get back as we're flying to
Brisbane tomorrow."

"Meet you in the gym at 5 am?" she asked with a
lift of her eyebrow.

"I'll be there," he said with a grin.

THE FOLLOWING day in Brisbane was similar to
Sydney. They were whisked across the city, going to
hospitals and meeting sick kids, and other such
events. It was exhilarating and exhausting.

Every moment that she was in the public view,
Paige was aware of everything she did from ensuring
she smiled and looked happy, to ensuring her clothes
were suitable. Every muscle in her body was strained
and on alert, as she was conscious about wanting to
ensure she did everything right for Sam. Every
moment of the day was scheduled by the organised
and meticulous Megan.

As the fake girlfriend, she was with Sam constantly, and they were often kissing, and holding hands.

Sam was acting, but Paige wasn't.

A couple of times she'd tried to speak to Megan privately, but it had been difficult with Sam or someone else interrupting them.

By the time they were in Adelaide, she noticed a change in Sam. He was snappy and disagreeable, even ignoring her at times in the limos or away from prying eyes. She wasn't sure what she'd done to evoke such a response, and she had no one to speak to about it. Besides, she didn't want to come across as a petulant teen, complaining that Sam was being cranky.

In the luxury van transporting them to the movie premiere, Megan retaliated. "Nice to see you taking your bitch pills every day." She glared at him before returning her focus to her mobile phone.

Paige's eyes widened with shock, but she said nothing.

"Shut up," Sam fired back.

Paige's breath hitched in her throat as the drama played out in front of her. It was the first time she'd seen him snap at staff.

"You're as much fun as a moody teenage girl

about to get her period," his PA taunted him, not even looking up from her phone.

"I could fire you," Sam said with a cold voice.

That made her look up. With a toss of her head, she said, "Go ahead, at least I wouldn't have to put up with you." Her face was deadpan, and Paige wasn't sure if she was serious or not.

A heavy silence settled in the car, and Paige squirmed in her seat watching with interest.

Sam finally broke the silence. "You're right, Megan. Delay what you can in Melbourne. Find me somewhere to go after Hobart. I need a break."

"You'll be taking a break *with Paige*, of course," she replied, her fingers typing frantically on her phone.

"Of course," he said with a strained voice.

And just like that, Paige felt her ribs tighten around her lungs. She and Sam were going away...together?

TWO DAYS PASSED and Sam was still moody around them all. She could see he was trying to make an effort, often apologising for a curt reply.

After the movie premiere in Hobart, she and Sam were whisked into yet another limo.

Megan leaned in. "I've booked you into a lake house, it's beautiful, quiet and remote. The fridge is stocked, and you'll have privacy. Your security team are staying nearby. We've got two actors who'll play you and Paige arriving in Melbourne in a couple of hours, so the media will believe you're there, not here. Enjoy the break and come back *happier*." She stepped back, closing the door so they were on their own.

The limo started to move and Sam closed his eyes, leaning back into the leather softness of the seat.

She touched his arm. "Do you want to talk to me?"

"No, later," he said closing his eyes. "It's a thirty-minute drive, I don't want to talk. Just leave me."

He closed his eyes and appeared to be dozing, so she looked out the window and watched the lights of the city fade as they drove away from it. Lost in her thoughts, she was surprised to find them arriving at the cabin. It was *a cabin* but it was beautiful. Despite the late hour and darkness, there were enough lights on to see the beautiful place that Megan had organised for them.

The security team was waiting for them.

"Everything is fine, we've checked it all. Enjoy your break. You know how to reach us," the tall beefy guy said, handing Sam a lanyard.

The security waved to them and headed to their car, and Paige watched them drive off down the private road. The limo driver had unloaded their bags for them, and then drove away, leaving them on their own.

The world was silent in the darkness, and she looked around admiring the serenity of the locale.

"Let's go," he said, grabbing their bags and walking to the cabin.

She trotted after him. Unlike him who walked straight ahead, not looking around, she took in the beauty of nature as her heart skipped with delight.

Inside, he dropped the bags with a thud. "There are two bedrooms, pick one. I'll take the other," he said. He walked off, opened the sliding glass door to the deck, and sat on the couch facing darkness, that she assumed was the river. The dark night and few lights made it difficult to tell.

He gave off a *leave me alone* vibe, so she decided to use some time to look at the house. The furnishings looked comfortable, yet were modern. She wheeled her bag through the house, looking at the bedrooms, which were comfortably furnished with plenty of throw rugs and pillows.

As each bedroom was the same size as the other, she took the room that appeared more feminine to her. Opening her bag, she found a pair of warm socks and happily wore them instead of shoes. Taking a blanket with her, she returned to the kitchen and found a bottle of wine, glasses, as well as a plate of cheeses and crackers in the fridge. Using a tray, she carried it all outside, before placing it on the table.

"I brought supper," she said. Returning to the lounge area, she grabbed an additional blanket and took it to Sam. "It's a little chilly, I thought you might like this."

"Thanks, that's thoughtful of you." He placed the throw across his lap, and returned his gaze to the dark night sky, still focussed on whatever was troubling him. Something had really upset him for him to be so pensive. The cheeky smile he usually wore had been replaced by a tired, defeated look with the skin around his eyes and cheekbones strained.

She unwrapped the cheese platter before opening the bottle of wine, pouring each of them a glass. Her fingers trembled slightly. It was just the two of them. Could she get him to talk, open up about whatever was troubling him?

Handing a glass to him she said, "Talk to me, what's going on? You're not yourself. I'm your friend, you can trust me."

He sipped the rich Merlot, not saying anything.

He continued to stare out across the darkened waters.

"It does help to talk," she encouraged him, hoping he'd share whatever it was that was bothering him.

"In my world, talking doesn't help, unless it's with your therapist," he said with a smile. His gaze still focussed on the water and not on her. He drank absently, and didn't seem to notice how good the wine was. It was almost as if he were drinking water, he just sipped not paying attention to the richness of the Merlot.

"Since Brisbane, you've been unhappy. What's happened? Are your parents okay?" Panic settled in her belly. She hoped nothing had happened to his family, she knew how close he was to them.

He waved her care away with a flick of his wrist. "They're fine. I'll be seeing them when we're back in Melbourne."

Her shoulders slumped with relief, knowing there were no issues with his family. But before she could dig deeper with his distress, she asked, desperate to know. "Do they know about me? I mean, that we're not really together?" She liked his parents, the few times she'd met them and would hate for them to be disappointed that their son hadn't really fallen for his teenage friend.

"I told them about it, obviously they know everything. I also didn't want them to get their hopes up about me settling down and them being grandparents." The tone of his voice was filled with resignation and he rubbed the back of his neck.

"They ask you a lot?" she asked in anticipation.

He turned his attention to her, from the black, night sky. "I'm their only son, their only child, of course they want me to marry and have children." He paused. "But. . .I just heard some disturbing news and it's made me wonder whether true love exists, especially in Hollywood."

She sucked in a sharp breath. "What happened?"

He ran his fingers through his hair before rubbing his eyes. He sat in his seat looking out, making her wonder if he was going to share his pain with her.

They sat there for a few minutes and she sipped her wine, not knowing what to say or do.

Eventually, Sam spoke. "I have a friend, you don't know him. He's in finance and super smart. I met him when I first moved to LA. He and his girlfriend, who has since become his wife, had moved there so she could pursue an acting career. She's beautiful and worked at a diner I used to go to." He cleared his throat. "They were from a small town and she had stars in her eyes, just like I did. We bonded over stories of making it big in Hollywood."

He blew out a long breath and he rubbed his chest, near his heart, with his palm. "And then I met her husband, and we just got on really well. I can't tell you how many dinners we've spent together, weekends and holidays. We even went on vacation to Mexico when I was in my early twenties. We've been tight ever since."

"Are they okay? Did something happen to them?" She nodded, blinking rapidly.

"Sort of. Tasha's career never really took off. She never got the break she thought she deserved. I was able to get her some bit-parts in my movies, but she wanted to be the star not have a minor role."

The skin across his cheeks was tight and strained, and she longed to hug him. But she held back, letting him speak. "Is she a good actor?" she asked tentatively.

"She is. . .but there are plenty of good actors in LA." He let out a long breath. "I told you, it's not an easy career. Harry, her husband, came to LA for her. He studied, worked long hours to provide for them, and is now working in a prestigious financial company."

Her heart started to hammer against her chest, in anticipation of what he was about to say. "And?"

"I've known them for twelve years, I thought they had a marriage that would stand against some of the decadent and degenerate issues I see in the industry. Harry has worked long hours so she can attend any audition or interview. Unlike others, she doesn't have a second job. He provides."

He closed his eyes and expelled a long breath. "He came home early the other day, not feeling well. He didn't bother telling Tasha, not thinking anything of it, and what happens? He finds his wife screwing his friend in…their…bed."

"What?" she snapped unable to believe what he'd just told her. "She betrayed her husband with his friend." She felt ill at his revelation. The poor guy. What a dreadful shock.

"Yep, and it may not have been the first time." He continued in a low voice.

"First time with the friend?—"

"No, he believes there have been others."

"Ohmygod, that's so awful." Compassion flowed through her, to the man she didn't know but was Sam's friend. No wonder he'd been so upset.

He rubbed his hands through his hair. "It is. I'm not just angry for my friend, but it's making me question my beliefs in marriage, fidelity, and the movie industry."

"It's one couple, not everyone in Hollywood," she shot at him.

"I know that. But, I've known them for years, I

truly believed what they had was true and *real* love." He shook his head. "I can't believe Tasha did what she did."

"Did she say why she did it? Not that it matters?"

He slouched. "This is the bit that disgusts me. She said Harry hadn't been paying her enough attention, and she needed to find solace with someone else."

"But didn't you say that he supported her? For years?" Her words tumbled from her lips.

"Yep. Even while he was studying, he worked weekends and nights so she could achieve her dream. And she thanks him by screwing his friend, and others." She could hear the disgust in his voice.

"No wonder you've been so upset lately. That's terrible news. Your poor friend."

His chocolate brown eyes darkened. "I'm angry, hurt and confused."

What a mess. Her heart ached for Harry, someone she didn't know who'd done so much for his girlfriend/wife. She knew so many actors had to work in shops and diners, and juggle auditions around that. Not Tasha. She'd been given everything, and had "thanked" her husband by being unfaithful. "What's your friend going to do?" A bitter tang soured her mouth.

He bowed his head. "He's moved out and is starting divorce proceedings."

"Poor guy." She really felt for Harry, no wonder Sam was so upset.

"Yep. He works for an international company so he's asked for a transfer. He'll take whatever he can, as long as it's away from her." The bitterness in the way he said *away from her*, made her eyes widen.

"Do they have an office here?" She pointed to the ground, meaning Australia.

He looked up and she could see the torment in his eyes. The pain and hurt he felt for his friend. "Actually, they do. If they agree, he'll move to either London, Hong Kong or Melbourne. He wants to get far away from her."

"I hope he can work things out," she said with a sigh. "And Melbourne's pretty far away from LA."

"Me too," he said with a deflated sigh.

"Thanks for sharing that with me, no wonder you've been so upset and low for the past couple of days. That must have been a real shock for you."

The world was so still around them that it was like they were the only ones on the planet. Not a breath of wind. Just a cool, still, dark night. Only the spray of stars and yellow sliver of the moon lit up the sky.

"It has been." He shook his head. "I'm also annoyed that I can't be there for him. I'm here promoting my movie, then I have the date to get through." He rubbed his eyes. "I want to get back to LA, and be there for Harry, and take him out for a beer, or three."

She sipped her wine. "They haven't announced the winner yet, or did I miss it."

"The winner has been contacted."

"Really? Can you tell me who it is?"

He lifted his brow. "You know I can't. All I can say is that they're from England."

"She must be so excited. Not only winning a date with you, but she gets to fly out to Australia. Has she decided where she wants her date?" When Paige had seen Sam promoting his charity event, she'd imagined them snorkelling together in the balmy, turquoise waters of Queensland followed by cocktails and dinner. Everything would be romantic from the flowers, mood lighting, and twinkle lights. She'd imagined it so many times, often daydreaming about she and Sam on a dream date.

"Yes," he said slowly, obviously holding back details.

"And?" she prompted, wondering if he'd share with her.

A tiny smile touched his lips but he lifted his brows and gave her an *I can't believe you asked me that question* look.

"Just thought I'd ask," she said, clarifying why

she'd done it. "She must be thrilled to be coming here to meet you."

There was merriment in his eyes, and she wondered what she'd said that was so amusing. "I hope so."

"What about me? Will that impact the date?"

"Not at all, this is a friendly date, not some seedy, sexual catch-up." He paused. "I didn't mean it like that. But, you know how it is. It's me spending the day with a fan, nothing more. But you will need to stay on as my fake girlfriend till I return to LA."

Disappointment weaved its way into her belly, and she felt her cheeks flush with dismay. Stupid really. She was a fake girlfriend. She really needed to remember that, and remind herself that Sam was acting. Those kisses had been fake, not real. "Okay, I'm assuming that I don't meet her." The light tone in her voice told him she was accepting of it all.

"You assumed right." He shot her a smile that was sincere. He stretched his arms above his head and yawned. "I'm so tired. I've been working a lot, and now I'm here flying to capital cities, meeting my fans and doing the PR necessary. And then this mess with Harry and Tasha."

"You probably need more than a couple of nights to recharge," she said, reassuring him.

"You're right but I have a new movie starting

soon. Besides, I can't afford to take off much time. I'd worry the whole time about missing out on roles," he confessed.

"You work in a ruthless industry. Can't you ensure you have more time between movies?" She suggested, before nibbling on a cracker.

"It depends when they start filming." He massaged the back of his neck, and she could see the strain the tour and Harry's issues were having on Sam. He needed this break.

"We have two nights and one day to relax. I want you to sleep in, not exercise and enjoy your time here. It's beautiful." She paused. "We can walk along the foreshore, or just read a book. There is so much food here, we won't starve." She instructed him, hoping he wouldn't mind that she was telling him what to do.

"Megan has been ever efficient," he said.

"She certainly has, and you should thank her by enjoying this. It's magical here." She nibbled another cracker with cheese.

The pallor in his skin was gone, and he seemed brighter...happier? Leaning across the table, he helped himself to some crackers, and topped off his glass of wine. "Tell me what you do? Not your work but how you spend your days."

"I don't go to movie premieres regularly or travel

first class or in private jets," she confessed with a chuckle. "My life is pretty boring compared to yours."

"Go on," he said, his hand gestured in the air, wanting to know more.

"I spend time with my parents, Rachel, and my sisters. I love my nephew, Lev, he's just too cute." She thought back to all the times they'd had together, kicking a ball in the park, feeding ducks at the park, fun at the local children's play centre.

"I'm surprised Paisley is a single mum—"

"That she didn't have an abortion?" She gasped, her hand covering her mouth. "Sorry."

"I didn't mean it like that. It seems so unlike her to have had a child outside marriage, she just seemed the type to fall in love, get married, and have a child."

"Unfortunately, she fell for the wrong guy, you know the bad boy." Paige made quotation marks in the air. "We love our nephew and mum fusses over him when she's not running the soup kitchen. She started one up a few years back, to help rehabilitate women who'd been in prison."

"Tell me about it," he said. He seemed relaxed now that he'd shared his pain with her. He sipped his wine, enjoying the platter of nibbles.

"Whilst the women were in prison, they would be bussed to my mum's kitchen, not at home but a place she rented. She taught these women how to peel and chop vegetables, about nutrition, and gave them life skills. The soup they made was distributed to those in need, but more importantly, the women learnt how to make food."

"That's a worthy idea," he said.

"It is. It means once these women are out of jail, they know how to cook, understand hygiene not just for themselves but also offers them opportunities for work." She could hear the excitement in her voice, she couldn't help it. She really admired her mother, and her contribution to those who needed her help. Not everyone wanted to work with criminals.

"I help out on weekends, when I can." She paused. "We also help children in need. We've recently started an after-school program where they're taught about nutrition, and how to chop vegetables." She was so proud of her mum. Children who knew about nutrition and cooking were less likely to eat too much fast food. She believed in moderation. Fast food was a treat, not something to be consumed every day. Healthy bodies meant a healthy mind. And she wanted these children to be achievers, in whatever field they chose to work in.

"Your mum has achieved all of this?" She could hear the surprise but also keen interest in his voice.

"She was a stay-at-home mum, and she loved it,

but as we got older, she wanted to do more, especially when we were at school." She explained. Once the four sisters had finished school, her mum needed to fill her days and find a way to help those who needed it.

"Once a month, we run a dog café." She told him, almost forgetting about the highlight of her month. She'd loved Poppy's idea from the beginning, and had supported her even when her mum wasn't sure about the idea.

He lifted his eyebrow. "Dog café?"

"I wish you could see it. There is an area out the back that is perfect. Poppy brings in the dogs and the kids play with them. We serve the children fruit smoothies and healthy cookies. It's so much fun."

"The dogs don't mind, with the children and fussing?"

"Not at all. It's Poppy's brainchild, and she knows what she's doing," she explained.

"It does sound like fun."

"Poppy finds the right dogs for the program. And we're all there to make sure everyone is safe. The children play and pet the dogs, and the dogs love the fun. Listen to this," she paused. "Last month, we did a wash-a-dog day." She chuckled remembering the fun they'd had. She'd even enjoyed spraying some of the kids with the water from the hose, since it'd been just a gloriously warm day.

"And you said your life was boring," he added, touching his nose. "You sound very interesting…and busy."

Her cheeks warmed from his compliment but she brushed it aside. "I didn't start the kitchen or dog café, I um, I, ah…just help out." She actually did more, like the weekly newsletters, organising the fundraising, and applying for community grants, to keep the program running and active.

He sipped his wine. "I'm sure there's more that you do. Tell me, if you could do anything, what would it be?"

She shrugged. "I don't know. I never thought about it." She was content with her life, her family and career. She'd never been lacking for anything. The only longing had revolved around Sam. And now that they'd been together, "dated" and shared some kisses, she was happy, truly she was.

"You sit in your family's shadow."

His comment surprised her and she looked up at him, not sure if he meant it as a compliment or not. "I like to think of it as supporting them."

He rolled his hand in the air. "But what's important to *you*?" He focussed on her. "You care for your nephew, helping your sister. You help at the kitchen, helping your mum. But what about what *you* want?"

Even after the clarification, she still wasn't sure how to answer. She felt she was genuinely lucky to have so much in her life. "Honestly, I don't know. I love my work, but I've never thought about doing anything on my own, like my mum and sister have done."

She fiddled with her glass and thought about it. If she really had to give an answer, she'd confess that she wanted to find love. Like him, she had parents with a strong, loving, supportive marriage and she hoped to find that kind of love with someone special. She'd thought it may blossom with Mike, but now she knew she had been kidding herself.

Mike was not the one for her. He hadn't helped once at the soup kitchen or dog café. There had always been a reason, but in hindsight, she knew that he just wasn't into helping those less fortunate than himself.

And recognising that made her realise why she could not be with Mike long term. Their values were not aligned. Shame, because despite him acting like a tosser with the media, he was an okay guy.

She kept her thoughts private, she wasn't going to share *that* with Sam.

"But look at you, and the work you do with those

teens, and the scholarships." She pointed out. Like her, he also liked helping others out.

"It's only a few hours each year, and to be honest, I'd like to do more," he confessed.

That surprised her. She was expecting him to want to cut back his hours, especially since he was so busy. "Like what?" she asked with genuine interest

He stretched in his seat, his elbows resting on the armrests, his fingers pressed together. "I'd like to mentor some young actors."

"That would be amazing," she said. "How lucky for them."

"The idea is great but practically, I don't know how I would do it." He let out a long breath. "If I'm not filming, I'm promoting or doing something related to my career. I have so little free time. I just don't want to commit to something that I can't give 100% to."

She nodded. "I agree. But it would be brilliant for you to help up-and-coming stars, what a break for them."

They sat, both caught up in their thoughts before she asked, "Tell me about your work?"

His head fell back. "Ugh. I love it, and hate it at the same time." His lips pressed together. "There are times I'm filled with disillusionment, and other times, I just love what I do."

183

She was surprised, not expecting him to feel that way. He was always so confident, and so assertive that she never expected he'd be plagued with doubts. "If you weren't an actor, what would you do... besides mentoring actors."

"I'm like you, I don't know."

Her heart skipped a beat as she remembered her lie. It's not like she could confess that if she didn't have her job, she wished they could be together, marry and have a happily-ever-after ending. Unlikely since his career consumed him, and now he'd lost faith in love, thanks to Harry and Tasha's broken marriage.

"You have the world at your feet." Her arm swept out dramatically. "Look at you. You've gone from Australian teen soapie star to one of Hollywood's most bankable stars."

"I do. But on the downside, I can't get a date on my own."

They chuckled at his retort.

"Touché," she said.

The rich wine had warmed her blood, and she snuggled into the woollen afghan, as the cool air caressed her cheeks. "It's so beautiful sitting here." She yawned. "Sorry, must be the wine."

He looked at his watch. "It's late, we have plenty of time to sit here tomorrow." He stood and collected the empty plates and glasses, before carrying them on a tray to the kitchen.

She retrieved the blankets and followed, before locking the doors.

She dumped them on the sofa, not bothering to fold them since they'd be using them tomorrow.

He turned towards her. She looked up at him, her heart rate quickening and her breathing rapid. She found it hard to remind herself that this was Sam, her friend not her celebrity crush and certainly not her fantasy. This was real life, not a romantic movie.

"Why are you looking at me that way?" He took a step towards her.

Her hands flew to her face and she cupped her cheeks. "What way? I don't know what you mean?" Her breathing became rapid.

"You're nervous. Your eyes betray you." He took her hand and placed his fingers across her pulse point feeling her erratic heartbeat. "Do I do this to you?"

She swallowed hard as nerves zigged up and down her spine. She wanted to howl out her defence. But she wasn't an actor. He'd even seen the betrayal in her eyes. "You're not just my friend, you're a Hollywood movie star. I-I, um, I can't just keep those two apart," she told him honestly.

"Why?" He held her hands, standing opposite her.

She could feel the warmth of his body, since he stood so close to her.

Her throat dried and she wanted to tell him the truth, but couldn't. She was shy and didn't have sass like her younger sisters. Her eyelashes fluttered as she debated on what to say.

He closed the gap between them, and lifted her hand so it rested on his chest near his heart. "If it helps, this is how you make me feel," he said.

She could feel his heart beating hard against his ribs. Her mouth opened but nothing came out.

"There is something special between us. You feel it, and so do I." He paused. "What I'm feeling is not very *friendly* but I don't want to ruin our friendship. I can't give you what you want."

"What do I want?" *Had her thoughts betrayed her?*

"A reliable, steady boyfriend who can be there for you. Someone who'll be there to support you when you're washing dogs, making soup for those in need, or watching TV on the couch."

He was exactly right. That was what she wanted. Mike never helped out at the dog café, but had been happy to watch TV with her...as long as it was a show that he liked.

"We're here together, *alone*," he stressed the word alone. "For the next two nights and tomorrow. I can't pretend that I'm not interested, but I don't want you to feel uncomfortable. I'm not making a move on you. You have my word." He paused. "We're friends, I don't want to hurt you."

She knew that. He was too kind and honest. The only way he'd hurt her would be unknowingly. Because when he returned to America, and she didn't see him except on the big screen, her heart would be broken. She adored him, wanted him in a way that was not friendly. But she couldn't do it. It would destroy her to give herself to him, knowing he couldn't commit to her.

She looked into his dark eyes filled with unfulfilled need. "I know. I trust you."

Her gaze took in his handsome face. The one that until recently had been the screen saver on her mobile phone. Could she snatch this moment of pure indulgence and walk away? She'd never had a one-night stand. She'd only ever had sex with a boyfriend she trusted, in a relationship.

She was almost thirty and wanted to meet someone special. She'd been looking for years, but she'd been inadvertently pushing them away because they weren't Sam.

And now Sam wanted her. She could make love with Sam...her private fantasy would come to life. But then what? He'd return to America, and she'd go back to her life.

The sensible side of her wanted to say no thanks, and go to her bedroom alone. The other side was delighted.

Would it be worth it? How would she and her crushed heart cope when he left her?

CHAPTER 10

"*I* can see the uncertainty in your eyes," he said.

"I-um." She didn't know what to say. Who said no to making love with Sam? Gosh, she was a fool. It wasn't that she didn't want to. She was scared. Scared of falling for him so hard that she would never recover. Rachel was right. She had placed Sam on a pedestal for so many years that once he returned to LA, leaving her, her heart would splinter in two.

Making love would add to the hurt. She'd give him her heart, knowing that he couldn't or rather wouldn't be able to give her what she wanted. She wanted the fairy tale, just like in *Pretty Woman*, where the hero suddenly realised that the heroine was the woman for him. Yep, pure fantasy.

It wasn't going to happen. Never would.

"I trust you, I do. Everything has happened so quickly." She tried to explain why she couldn't do it. Would he understand?

"We're friends, nothing is going to change that." He kissed her nose. "Good night, sleep well."

He walked away from her, and Paige's lungs emptied with frustration and longing.

She heard the door to his room close and she was alone. It was better this way... right?

She groaned aloud, wishing she was more like Phoebe. Phoebe took charge of her life in a determined way. If a guy who she admired wanted her, she'd go with him. She wouldn't be indecisive like her.

Because of the intensity of the past few days, she should've been exhausted but her mind was too active and she knew she wouldn't be able to sleep.

A selection of novels had been left on a bookshelf and she perused them, taking a political thriller written by a well-known author. Reading always relaxed her. She'd read till her mind emptied and she felt tired. It's not like she had work the following day. Reading late into the night was one of her guilty pleasures.

Plonking herself on the comfy couch, she

wrapped herself in the warm blanket and started to read.

Half an hour later, having been engrossed in her book, Paige stood, stretched her legs but was still wide awake. She lit the fire, and poured herself another glass of wine. With the windows looking out to the dark water, she snuggled back under the fleecy blanket, enjoying the quiet time and relished the opportunity to be alone.

SAM LOOKED AT THE CLOCK. Three in the morning and he was awake. Bugger. His body throbbed with need, and he knew what he ached for. Paige.

Paige! He couldn't believe that he no longer saw her as a friend, a buddy, but someone he wanted with a longing that was keeping him from sleep.

How had that happened?

Was it all the kisses and caresses, over the past few days?

Sharing secrets?

Suddenly his body had become attuned to her in such a way that he'd never felt like this with another woman.

He loved spending time with her, she was easy to talk with and so easy going. He liked that she steered clear of any discussion of gossip or nastiness. She was sweet but sexy as hell. He hated that she couldn't see how gorgeous she was. Her sister, Phoebe, was an international model, but she did nothing for his libido. Paige, on the other hand, with her slim curves, cheeky humour and pretty features made his body tighten with want and desire.

When he'd first seen her last week wearing that sexy, black leather combination he'd almost swallowed his tongue. She'd blossomed into a stunning woman who not only interested him, but made his heart race. Something no woman had done…till now.

But he couldn't have a relationship with her. She lived here and he lived in LA. He travelled constantly.

If Harry and Tasha's marriage couldn't last, what hope did he have in being with someone who didn't understand the industry? Paige wouldn't last a minute in his world.

He blew out a long breath of frustration.

Even his parents had moved away from it. The industry was not for them. They'd ensured he was settled with a reliable manager and well connected. Then, in his early twenties, his parents had returned to Melbourne, relieved to be home and close to their friends once more. They'd hated LA.

He understood their need to return to Australia, even though he missed them so much.

The house was quiet, and he assumed Paige was asleep. Standing, he shivered in the cool night air, and grabbed a robe to cover his naked body.

He padded to the kitchen, intending to have a drink of water but was surprised to see Paige asleep on the sofa. Wrapped in a blanket, a book had fallen to the floor, and the fire was going. It was one of those electric fires that looked real.

Fast asleep, her head was tilted in a funny position, and he was concerned she'd wake with a sore neck. He walked to her and took a moment to watch her sleep. Peaceful. Her pretty face was content as she slept deeply.

His finger trailed down her cheek. "Paige, wake up."

She smiled in her sleep, but her eyes didn't open.

"Paige, honey, you need to get up." He used a louder voice so she'd awaken and could go to bed, by herself.

She didn't stir. She must be tired.

"Wake up," he said.

She murmured his name, but her eyes didn't open.

"Paige," he said before brushing his lips against hers. "You need to get up."

"Sam," he heard her sigh, as her lashes fluttered open. "What are you doing here?"

He started to explain that she'd fallen asleep in the lounge area. "I found you—"

"You came for me," she said with a sigh. "You came to me." She lifted her hands, gripping his neck so their faces were only centimetres apart. "Sam." She lifted her head and brushed her lips back against his.

His body stiffened. He hadn't intended for anything to happen, except for him to send her to bed…alone.

"Sam," she said, lifting her head so they could kiss.

Her soft lips clung to his own and he melted with the longing and desire. His blood warmed with the feel of her clutching on to him and his resolve melted.

Just one kiss, he assured himself. Just one kiss and then he'd break them apart. The temptation was too great. The scent of her hair, the press of her lips against his was all too much. He kissed her back.

Their lips met, and it was like their first kiss by the beach. It started as a few tentative kisses, sweet and welcoming.

But then her mouth opened, urging him on. She tugged at the lapels of his robe, drawing him close.

He broke their kiss for a moment, and before long he was lying on top of her, using his arms to support his weight.

The sweet, coconut scent of her hair teased his nostrils, and he deepened their kiss. Their tongues tasted each other, and her hands ran up and down his back.

They kissed and kissed. And then suddenly, the urge to devour her overcame him. His lips trailed along her cheek to her ear. He ran his tongue along the rim and smiled as she groaned with delight.

He sucked the lobe, before pressing urgent kisses along her neck. The taste of her, so sweet.

Her eyes widened. "Sam? Is this really you?"

Concern spiked in his belly. Was this all part of a dream? "Paige?"

Her gaze met his. "Your kisses woke me. Are you really kissing me?"

It was more that she was kissing him, but he wasn't going to correct her, not when he could see the worry in her eyes.

"Do you want me to stop?" He had to ask. He'd stop if she asked, but he hoped that she didn't want to.

She grinned in return. "No way." She pressed her lips against his. "It's not often I get woken by a sexy man kissing me."

"I don't want you to get the wrong idea," he started to say.

Rubbing herself against him she said, "I think I like the *wrong* idea."

His body tensed as her hands ran up and down his back.

With difficulty, he lifted himself off her. The sofa was not comfortable for what he had in mind, and if they were going to make love, he wanted it to be special.

He stood next to her and held out his hand, and helped her to her feet.

His robe had fallen open and he caught her looking at him. Her gaze swept from his chest, all the way down to his toes.

"You like?" His voice was thick with emotion.

"Hell yeah, I do," she said, tugging him to her so she could kiss him again.

The kisses became more urgent, and his hands tingled with anticipation of pleasuring her. Grabbing the blanket, he laid it on the floor in front of the fire.

She watched him through hooded eyes.

Her lips were full, and looked well kissed. He couldn't wait to kiss her all over.

They stood facing each other, he in his robe, and she in her jeans and sweater. She reached down and tugged off her sweater and top, and stepped out of her pants, so she stood in front of him in a pretty bra and panty set.

The fire lit up her smooth skin and his fingers ached to caress her. "You're so beautiful." He took a step towards her. One hand on her waist, and the other on her shoulder. He kissed her, really kissed her, like a man desperate. He couldn't help it. Her taste. The soft press of her lips, and the tiny groans she made urging him on.

"I want you," she breathed into his ear as her hand came up and ran across the planes of his chest. Her fingers trailed down, and she took hold of his erection. She rubbed up and down and he groaned with her audaciousness. He was hard. So hard that he thought he would pass out from wanting her.

She cupped him, her fingers caressing him to the point that he was about to explode.

"Take me now," she whispered before nibbling his ear. Her tongue ran along the rim of his ear and he shuddered.

"Not yet my beautiful," he said, pressing kisses along her bare shoulder.

As much as he'd love to just take her, he held back. Not yet. He wasn't some caveman. He wanted to give her pleasure, and watch her head roll back as his tongue and fingers brought her first of many orgasms. They only had a short time together and he intended in making it incredible for both of them.

Her hands came up and slipped off his robe, so that it pooled on the floor at his feet.

"You're so hot," she heard him murmur as they came together to kiss once more. He gripped her bottom, pulling her towards him.

He started to kiss her shoulder and them down her chest so that his mouth covered her nipple and he sucked hard, through the lace of her bra. In seconds he'd unsnapped it, and tossed it aside. Taking a moment, he looked at the perfect pink nipples on her small breasts. Perfect. His hands cupped her breasts before he sucked one nipple to a tight bud.

He tugged her towards him, and lay her on the blanket, so they were side by side. He took that moment to look at her glorious body laid out for him, like a feast. He took in her beautiful, natural perfection from her flat belly to long legs. Legs that he couldn't wait to have wrapped around his waist.

"You're beautiful, every exquisite inch of you," he said, before tugging her panties off and throwing them behind her.

He lay on top of her and kissed her. He spent time cupping her breasts and kissing them before he made his way down her belly, and then lower. He slid down her body, his mouth watered thinking about how he'd pleasure her.

With her knees bent, he moved his mouth to her most intimate spot, and blew lightly. She shivered in response and he smiled. His mouth came down and he kissed her, kissed her most secret spot.

"Sam," she cried out, her voice thick with desire.

His tongue licked the length before he licked and sucked her folds till she was panting, and begging for completion. Using his finger, he traced the movements of his tongue. Using his fingers and mouth, he brought her to almost finishing before he stopped and she cried out, begging him.

"Soon, my lovely," he said before inching his way to lie beside her. They faced each other as his fingers trailed down to the junction of her legs. "I want to watch you come," he said. His fingers started again to trace her lips. He watched her suck a deep breath as he inserted one finger, then two.

He massaged her gently.

Her back arched. "I need to come," she begged. "Sam please."

His mouth captured her nipple and licked it, as his fingers worked on her.

Her breathing grew rapid, and she repeated his name over and over. Then he shifted slightly so he massaged her secret nub, and she screamed out his name as she clenched hard around his fingers. All the while, he watched her beautiful face while she came and came.

And when she lay spent against the blanket, biting her lip, he knew he was crazy for her. He wanted her, body and soul.

He had no idea how things would work beyond Melbourne, but she was special and he wanted this time with her.

For the time being, he intended to pleasure her for as much time as he could while they were here, away from the prying media.

PAIGE LAY ON HER BACK, her heart thumping hard as her breathing started to slow. Wow, was the only word she could think of. She'd never come as hard as she had with Sam's magical touch, and now she wanted more, so much more.

Not caring about what was going to happen in the light of day, she wanted to focus on the joy of them coming together.

She was a realist. It would be one night or more, and then they would go their separate ways. But until then, she wanted to enjoy every decadent second.

She knew that her heart was going to be ripped in two when he returned to America, but now, she didn't care. She wanted him with a desperation that made her shudder.

His fingers drew lazy circles across her breasts.

She turned to him and smiled. "That was amazing," she confessed.

"I'm glad you enjoyed it," he said before brushing his lips across hers.

"Is this weird for you?"

"What do you mean?"

"Friends having sex?"

"Yes. No." He brushed his lips across hers before tonguing her nipple to a tight bud. "If I said I regretted it, I'd be lying."

He moved up and rested on his arm so they were face to face.

"I don't regret it, but I will regret it if we don't finish what we started," she said with a newfound boldness.

"I need to get us some protection," he said. "Back in a sec." He stood and walked to his room, returning with a handful of foil packets.

"I'm not going to be able to walk tomorrow if you use all of them," she joked.

"I was in a hurry to get back to you, I just grabbed a handful." He lay back on the blanket facing her, his finger trailed along her cheek. "I want you."

"I want you, too," she said before she kissed him. She kissed with a hunger that she'd never felt before. The longing, the wanting was so strong that she couldn't stop it even if she wanted to.

She inched down his body, pressing kisses along his flat belly. Further down, she reached her goal. He stood to attention, almost waiting for her touch.

Her fingers tentatively touched him again, and he groaned. She took her time to caress him before she lowered her mouth over his length. This time he let out a guttural groan and she smiled. Using her fingers and lips she pleasured him, loving the hard feel in her mouth. She looked up to see his head thrown back and his arms clenched above his head.

Lifting her head, she reached to the table and grabbed the first of many packets she hoped to use. Within seconds she'd sheathed him, sat up and lowered herself onto his rock-hard length.

Inch by delicious inch, she moved slowly, loving the intimate feel of him.

"Paige," he groaned.

Their gazes met and he didn't look away until he was fully immersed in her.

She ran her fingers along the flat planes of his belly before she leaned over to lick his nipples. His eyes shut, but he gripped her hips while moaning her name.

Back in a seated position, she rocked a little, feeling him deep inside of her. She let out an expletive, loving how amazing it felt to be connected to him.

His hands came up to cup her breasts and his fingers gently teased her nipples.

Closing her eyes, she started to rock more, before she slid up and down his impressive length.

"Sweetheart, that feels so good," he said, before his hands rested on her hips.

"You want it faster," she said.

"I'll take it any way you want," he said.

She bit her lip and then started to ride him... hard. Back and forth to the rhythm of their steady breathing.

The pleasure built and she greedily wanted more. All she could focus on was the intense sensations of them united. She became wild, riding him hard, crying out his name.

And then his fingers touched her intimately, she screamed out as an orgasm tore through her. "Sam, Sam, Sam."

She opened her eyes to see his eyes glazed with passion, and soon after he bit his lip. "Finally," he groaned, as he pumped into her, hot and hard. He came and came.

She collapsed on top of him, sweaty, breathing heavily and joyously fulfilled.

With difficulty, she lifted herself off him and collapsed on the blanket, as their breaths and the heavy scent of lovemaking filled the room.

"That was amazing," she said.

"You're amazing," he said, before he kissed her mouth hard.

HE GOT up and disposed of the used condom. Despite the intensity of them coming together, he was not tired. In fact, he was on high alert. He wanted her again, and then he was going to have her again. The scent of her skin was driving him crazy and all he could think about was pleasuring her.

He lifted her to standing. "Come here. Do you know how sexy you are? I want to watch you, it turns me on."

He sat, and she watched as he sheathed himself. A rip of need tore through him as he watched her lick her lips.

Holding out his hand, he beckoned her to him. She

came willingly, lowering herself onto him again, but this time, they were face to face. Joined intimately, they spent time kissing, and touching each other.

It was the most intimate lovemaking he'd ever experienced. Sure, he'd had lovers before, but he'd never done or wanted to do something so special.

They pleasured each other while locked together. He kissed her breasts, tongued them and used his fingers to drive her crazy with need.

He nibbled her ear and ran his tongue across the lobe.

And then he kissed her, over and over, till they were both panting in need.

She started to rock against him.

"No, not yet."

"I'm dying here, I need to come," she pleaded, her skin flush with desire.

"Do you trust me?"

She looked at him and smiled. "Look at us? We're connected as lovers." Her gaze travelled down to where they were joined.

"Get up from me," he said with difficulty.

She slowly lifted herself with a pretend frown.

"I'm going to make you come so hard," he said, kissing her flat belly.

"Put your hands here," he pointed to the headrest

of the sofa. "And widen your legs." She did so. "Perfect."

His hands ran over the smooth expanse of her back, and then across the globes of her toned bottom. Stunning. She really was so beautiful, so natural, that his heart felt ready to burst out of his rib cage with need.

His hands caressed her intimately, and he felt her shudder against his fingers. He did it again, and again.

His hands came around her body and cupped her dangling breasts as he pressed kisses across her back.

She moaned with delight, and he became harder, if that were at all possible.

He kissed her neck and licked along her shoulder, his hands gently massaging her breasts.

As her breathing grew more rapid, one hand lowered to caress her, feeling her ready and waiting for him, he shifted his stance. Gripping her hips, he inched into her slowly.

"Omygawd," she cried out. "I'm going to come."

"Not yet babe," he said.

He withdrew and then plunged into her. She screamed out his name urging him on, begging for more. He did it over and over, till he felt her muscles contract around him. And then, when he knew she was spent, he finally allowed himself to finish.

He collapsed on top of her, knowing he was too heavy, but too tired to move. "Gimme a sec."

"That was amazing," she said. "But I need to lie down."

With difficulty, he lifted himself, disposed of the condom and returned to her. Turning off the fire with a flick of the switch, he held out his hand. "Fireplaces may be romantic but I'm not sleeping on the floor. Come with me."

"Sleeping in a bed with you sounds perfect," she said with a smile.

Hand in hand, they walked to his room, and he helped her into his bed. Tugging her close, her head settled on his shoulder, and his arm protectively came around her.

Within seconds, he was fast asleep, feeling happy and content...for the first time in a long time.

CHAPTER 11

*P*aige woke to find something heavy on her hip. She opened her sleepy eyes to see Sam's face inches away from hers. His eyes were closed, and he looked to be in a deep sleep.

The last few hours came rushing back at her, and how wantonly she'd been with him.

She'd never been so upfront and forthright with a man before.

Holy smokes, the sex had been incredible and she was sure she was about to self-combust with need. He'd made her come so intensely that she was sure her lungs would explode. She'd been pretty noisy as well, and was glad they were isolated, and that especially the security detail wasn't nearby.

She blushed as she recalled her enthusiasm with Sam, and also how upfront she'd been with him.

They were friends, and yet quickly they'd moved to the "friends having sex" zone. How could they go back after last night? She tasted him, and kissed most of his hard, toned body.

She had no regrets.

She knew it would hurt when he left, but until then, she just wanted to be with him. She wanted to experience the tenderness and raw lovemaking they'd shared.

She should be tired and needing rest but she was wired.

It was still early, as though the world had not yet woken. As she lay there deciding whether to get up or not, Sam's arms came around her anchoring her naked body to his. "Don't go," he murmured in her ear. "It's too early to get up."

Decision made. She snuggled into the pillowy softness of the bed, and with the warm, hard press of Sam's body against her back, she finally drifted back to sleep.

SHE'D SLEPT IN. Something she never did...but could get used to. After a quick shower, and dressed in her favourite jeans and sweater, she watched Sam make her breakfast.

"I certainly love a man who knows his way

around the kitchen," she cooed, watching him sauté the mushrooms and spinach. "I'm a terrible cook."

"Lucky for you then that I'm good. Besides, I'm famished. You wore me out last night," he said with a cheeky grin.

She felt her cheeks warm remembering how good it had been. "Last night was amazing."

He stopped cooking and looked up at her, his gaze seemed to undress her. "It was amazing."

Their gazes met and she stared at him, as lust pummelled through her.

He chuckled. "Don't worry, I'm not some caveman, breakfast first."

"I'd hate to waste all this cooking," she said.

"Finish setting the table, as it will be ready soon." He walked over and playfully flicked her bottom with a tea towel.

She squealed and raced around the kitchen bench.

"And don't forget the juice, glasses, and toast."

She saluted him. "Yes, sir." She took a moment to watch him. Dressed in denim jeans and a T-shirt, he looked so darn sexy, even his bare feet were sexy. And darn her noticing.

Minutes later, she had the table set, the blinds were up and the wide windows showcased a large expanse of water, extending out.

"It feels like we're the only ones here, don't you think?"

"We aren't, but yes."

"Is there security around?"

"They are, but they'll leave us alone. It's unlikely we'll be disturbed." He paused. "A whole day to ourselves, however will we entertain ourselves?" His lips twitched with amusement.

"We could read," she suggested with a shrug.

"We could. Are you sore after last night?" The playfulness was gone from his voice.

"A little," she said with honesty.

"We'll take it easy today and later on, I'll kiss it better." His deep, sexy voice made her shudder with need.

She bit her lip, thinking about how much she was looking forward to him doing that. "I heard kissing helps things feel better, so yes, that would be nice."

"Let's eat." He pointed to the cooked breakfast he'd made.

They carried their plates of poached eggs, spinach, mushrooms, avocado and toast to the table. They sat opposite each other, and for a few minutes, just enjoyed eating.

"These mushrooms are amazing. I love the herbs in them. Is there anything you can't do?"

"I'm terrible at math, chemistry, and physics. Do

you know of anyone who could help me?" His face was all innocence, but she was totally mesmerised. He was hot, and he was even hotter when they were making love. Watching him come last night had been a big turn-on.

"I may," she said. Her insides melted into goo as he smiled at her. Yep, he still had that effect on her, even after an incredible night of lovemaking.

She spread the avocado on her toast, and topped it with the sautéed mushrooms, and took a large bite. "So good."

"I'm glad."

"Tell me," she said between bites. "What's it like being famous?"

He lowered his cutlery. "Honestly, when I first made it big, I loved it. I mean, who wouldn't?" He paused. "I had studios wanting me, and companies using my image to promote my products. You can feel like you're very special and the king of the world, so to speak."

"And the women?" Her tummy tightened, wanting to know and also at the same time, not wanting to know.

"Initially, it was flattering to have women come up to me, giving me their numbers. I mean, I'm a guy. Who wouldn't want that?" He shrugged and she stifled a grin.

"But?" She leaned towards him, interested to know more.

He blew out a long breath then sipped his juice. "Most, from my experience, want something from me. Perhaps, they want to say they slept with me, or they want to sell a story, or they hope they'll accidentally get pregnant..." He made quotation marks in the air when he said accidentally.

She stopped and thought about what he said. "No wonder you were so angry when you thought I'd set you up."

"The last person I expected to betray me would be you." He paused. "I know you're not like that, but I was tired, jet-lagged, and I had my support team berating me for being so stupid."

"I'm sorry." She placed her toast on her plate and looked at him. "I'm sorry, I really am. And I'm sorry for the whole fake girlfriend thing you had to do."

"It hasn't been a hardship." He gave her a grin that made her feel all mushy inside. "I've enjoyed the past few days. I trust you." He paused. "And I don't trust many people."

His compliment warmed her skin, and reminded her that they had a past, even if it was a platonic one. "It must be hard not knowing if someone likes you for you, or as you the star."

He nodded. "Exactly. But, with you, I know you like me for me."

She bit her lip as a lump of longing became wedged in her throat. She may wish for him to suddenly see her as gorgeous, and someone to be with. But the realistic side of her knew that wouldn't happen.

He needed to be with someone who was just as fabulous as he was. Only a model or actor could understand the needs of his demanding career, and could sashay down the red carpet looking effortlessly stunning.

Skating she could do. Sashaying she could not.

As a teen, he was a great guy. And now as a man, he still had all those qualities that she liked about him then; honest, dependable, kind, funny, honourable. She could see herself falling for him. Him. Sam. Not the star, but him as a man.

Her hand motioned towards the large windows, to distract her from her thoughts. "This place is gorgeous. I could sit and watch the view all day."

He smiled in return. "We should go for a walk along the beach after. It's cold outside, but we'll layer up."

"Sounds perfect," she cooed. "And then after, we'll play chess," she said with determination.

"Forget it," he said slicing his hand through the air. "You always beat me."

She grinned. "Fine, we'll play Monopoly. There are heaps of board games we can spend the day playing."

"Forget the board games, there are some other *games* I want to play with you," he said in a low voice.

She involuntarily shivered. "I, um, would like that. . .a lot."

They finished their breakfast, then had a coffee sitting outside on the patio bundled up warm under a large blanket.

She would never forget being away with Sam. Obviously, the lovemaking had been incredible, but she was enjoying this time to reconnect with him. She loved hearing his stories of his on-set antics and the fun he had with the crew. And he shared stories about learning how to ride a horse, duel with swords and learn to stride in boots.

"You looked very dashing in those movies. I must say seeing you and other actors all dressed up in historical garb makes me wish for the return of breeches and knee-high boots."

"I prefer my jeans, if that's okay," he said giving her a dazzling smile. The dazzling smile that had been captured on numerous billboards and social media pics.

"Tell me more about you?" He nuzzled her neck.

Her forehead crinkled. "Me?" She blew out a large breath for dramatic effect. "My life is pretty boring compared with yours. I mean, I don't date anyone famous. No one is going to film the work I do, and my love life…I reckon it's pretty pathetic."

"Tell me," he said. "I promise not to share."

"I've never had much luck in the boyfriend department. I mean, I'm on the geeky side, I love to skate, and I'm very tall." Wasn't that the understatement of the year.

"And?"

She rolled her eyes. "This from the man who can have any woman he wants."

He didn't answer her but rather his gaze remained on her, waiting for her to tell him what he wanted to know.

"I'm pretty easy going with my *list* for a potential boyfriend, but apart from the obvious—being kind, thoughtful, not abusive—I just want someone who's taller than me," she admitted, feeling like a total tosser, and wishing they could go back to kissing.

He leaned over and kissed her nose. "Come on, let's walk and then you can make me another coffee."

THEY WALKED HAND IN HAND, and Sam felt a wave of contentment settle over him. For the first time that he could remember, he was feeling relaxed and happy.

Usually, he was worried about something. There was always something to think about, be concerned about. And now, here he was in a remote area in Tasmania with Paige. He'd never felt like this with anyone else. The sex had been amazing, but it was more than that. He was enjoying his time with her. He wasn't thinking about the lines he needed to memorise, the workouts he needed to do with his trainer, or the events he needed to attend, to be "seen."

He couldn't remember the last time he'd slept in, made breakfast and just relaxed. There was always something to do. Yet here, alone with Paige, he finally had time to rest and recharge.

He'd always adored Paige. Not only smart but she was cute, funny, and interesting. But there was nothing cute about how incredibly responsive she'd been to his touch last night. She'd exploded in his arms, and he'd loved every second.

He couldn't wait to have her back in his bed tonight or even this afternoon. He intended to pleasure her over and over again.

With less than a week left in Australia, he still

wanted to spend time with his family before he returned to Hollywood. Back to his chaotic life, the life he loved…right?

As he walked along the sandy beach, the sky clouded, the waves lapping at the shore, and the cool air brushing his face, the sun and bright lights of Hollywood seemed very far away.

He took a deep breath.

Once he was back home, he'd be back to his usual self. This moment of reflection, this consideration of his lifestyle and career was only happening because he was away from it.

Surely once he returned to his home, was on the phone to his agent, and attending functions, this time away would be a distant memory.

His mind flickered to the parties and movie premieres, the air kissing and chitchat that focussed on fashion, affairs, and awards. He'd prefer to have Paige there. She was far more interesting and fun to be around. But that wouldn't happen. Her life was here, and his was there.

She'd hate Hollywood, just like his parents had. They'd tolerated it enough for him to be settled.

Even if Paige came to LA with him, what would she do? She'd be bored, lonely, and she'd hate it.

If Harry and Tasha's marriage couldn't survive the industry demands, how could he expect Paige to deal with it? She was so sweet. As his girlfriend, she'd be scrutinised by the media. Every outfit she wore would be assessed by the fashion police. Yet another reason for Paige to hate LA.

No, he'd never do that to her. He loved and respected her too much.

They'd spend this time together...and then they'd go their separate ways.

And that would be best for *her*. He only wanted what was best for her.

A FEW HOURS LATER, Sam closed his eyes as his breathing regulated. They'd made love on the sofa, in front of the fireplace and now in bed. She curled up against him, and his fingers brushed the soft skin of her shoulder.

"I'm not having sex again until you feed me," she whispered into his ear before she ran her tongue along the rim.

He shuddered, aching to have her again. They'd taken it slow all afternoon as he hadn't wanted to hurt her. Every time they'd had sex, it had been wonderful. He loved how they'd come together in a way he'd found unique yet at a deeper level. Something he'd never experienced before. Their connection, both on a friendship and sexual level, had shaken him to his core.

It was so different from anything he'd ever had with a woman, and he pushed away the unfamiliar feelings, unready to explore them. It was too new and too much to think about.

For the first time, in years, he was relaxed and truly happy. He'd let his guard down and enjoyed time with Paige. He'd ignored his messages and social media, and allowed himself to be with her fully.

Again, a first for him.

The demands of his job and his public profile meant he was often thinking about sharing some snippet of his day with his fans. But for this short time in Tasmania, he wanted to be selfish, and just be with Paige.

No social media posts. No emails. No scripts to read.

Just him and Paige.

He tugged her close, his hand settled on her waist before he pressed a kiss against her lips. Perfect.

"We'll rest and then I'll make you dinner." With contentment flowing through his veins, he closed his eyes and allowed himself to fall asleep.

. . .

THE FOLLOWING morning Sam was tying the laces of his sneakers. His brief vacation was over, and he was needed in Melbourne. A wave of disappointment had initially washed over him that he was returning to "life." Another day or so would've been perfect. But he'd loved this break, and had time to reflect on Harry and Tasha's fall-out.

Paige had listened, while he talked.

The pain he'd been carrying had dissipated, and he was feeling better than he had in a long time.

He made a mental note to buy gifts for his staff, a thanks for putting up with his cranky mood a few days earlier.

He stretched his arms above his head, feeling energised. And it wasn't just from the shower sex they'd had.

He couldn't stop grinning that he'd been the one to introduce Paige to the joys of sex in the shower. She was the perfect height for him, and her enthusiasm had made it even better.

Great sex. Friendship. Decent sleep. The perfect combination for the past two nights and day, and he felt a million times better than he had when they'd arrived.

The sex. How good had the sex been? Unbelievable.

They'd been amazing together, and his fingers

itched to caress the soft skin behind her ear. She was the most beautiful woman, most responsive to his touch, that he'd been with.

He knew he was going to miss her a lot when he returned to LA. And not just the sex. She understood him in a way that his staff and friends didn't. She called a spade, a spade. And didn't sugar coat things because he was a star. He knew he could trust her. And there were few people he trusted.

He stood, grinned.

He felt so good, so happy.

Nothing was going to ruin his good mood. Nothing.

They'd already had breakfast and soon the security would collect them, drive them to the airport where a private plane would fly them to Melbourne.

And then it would all start again.

But for now, he wanted to enjoy this last hour. Time alone.

Whistling, he walked into the lounge area and found Paige hunched over her phone, typing a message, her face blanched.

"Paige?" His stomach twisted knowing that something bad was about to erupt and ruin his perfect morning.

She looked up, and he could see the upset and disappointment etched across the tightness in her jaw. She pressed her lips together, and then said, "I'm sorry."

"About what?" The dread of his happy mood being interrupted made him press his lips together with annoyance.

She bit her lip, as though debating what she was going to say. After a few seconds which felt like minutes, she said, "It's Mike. I just turned my phone on." Her lower lip was trembling. "He's carrying on. But I reckon he's doing it for the media—"

"What now?" He wished he didn't have to deal with this. He was in such a good mood, couldn't it wait? But it couldn't. Paige's lip trembled and he knew they needed to deal with her ex.

"He's done this interview piece about him being the wounded lover, discarded for the Hollywood star." She groaned dramatically. "Tosser."

He held out his hand. "Let me see it." Not that he was interested in it, but wanted to know who'd run the story. He was sure his PR team were onto it.

She turned her phone and placed it in her lap. "You don't need to read it." There was shame and hurt all over the face, and he could see lines of disappointment around her eyes, that hadn't been there an hour ago.

An hour ago, she'd been in a playful mood, talking and laughing as they cleaned up after breakfast. The Paige in front of him looked shaken by the media reports, she'd just read.

This was the reason why he didn't read such rubbish. It was always wrong, or perhaps a semblance of truth woven into untruths.

He'd stopped reading the tabloids years ago, and left any issues to his staff to manage. Not that there had been any. He was careful in who he slept with, who he spoke to, and who he trusted.

Paige, on the other hand, was experiencing his life for the first time. It couldn't be easy for her.

He'd manage it, help her through it. Yet another reason why he couldn't see them being together more than a short time. The pressure of his life would tear them apart. He couldn't even consider asking her to be with him.

His parent's marriage had suffered, and look at his best friend. Crap. Harry and Tasha. Another casualty.

Good marriages that had been impacted by the demands of the movie industry. Even if Paige wanted to move to Hollywood, he knew the constant scrutinising of their relationship would drive a divide between them.

He blew out a long breath of frustration.

The disappointment had dulled her beautiful eyes, and he hated that some media report did that.

"You do know that I have my own phone, and can access the article myself," he said in a smug tone.

He couldn't imagine what had been published, and knew it couldn't be that bad. Honestly. Paige was as squeaky clean as they came. The grain of truth was probably embellished to create an article. He could dismiss it, she couldn't. It was all too new for her.

A look of guilt crossed her face. "It's embarrassing, please don't read it. I can't bear for you to see it, especially after what we've shared." She gulped hard, and he could see she was worried about his reaction to the piece.

Yep, she was so new to this, unlike him who didn't care.

"I get rubbish printed about me all the time. It's fine," he said with a reassuring tone. "I don't even read it, my team does. Do you know how much has been printed about me over the years?"

She cocked an eyebrow at him. "A lot?"

"Yep. And mostly good. But a story is a story."

She shook her head. "Maybe for you, but I've never been in the papers and certainly not linked to a Hollywood movie star. I'm feeling sick knowing my friends, my family, and my work colleagues can read this about me." She pointed to her phone. "It's humiliating."

Her head bowed, and he walked over to her.

"It's okay. No one will believe it. I'll threaten them with suing for slander against your good name. We'll manage this together." He put his arms around her, and could feel her trembling. "Paige, what's going on?"

Couldn't she trust him to see that he wasn't worried about what was printed in the media? He knew her. He trusted her.

Whatever it was, wasn't going to change his opinion of her.

"That's the problem. You can't sue, because what they've printed is the truth," she cried out before burying her face in his shoulder.

CHAPTER 12

*P*aige wanted to vomit and hide in shame. The mini-vacation away with Sam was ruined and she wanted to cry out for the injustice of it all. How could Mike do this to her?

Mike was hurt by her so-called betrayal and had used the media to lash out at her. He'd accomplished all that he wanted. She was hurt and humiliated. She hoped he'd enjoyed his brief moment as a celebrity because she would never forgive Mike for doing what he'd done.

"Tell me what it says, I promise I won't laugh," Sam said with a reassuring tone, sitting beside her.

"I feel like a teenager again with the mean girls laughing at me. But this time, I'm an adult, and all Australians are lapping up this drama. I mean, look at you, and look at me. The media is loving this." She turned away so he couldn't see the unshed tears in her eyes.

"Tell me what he said, and I promise to support you." His arm came around her shoulders, and he drew her near.

The citrus scent of his aftershave, and the strength of his muscles relaxed her resolve not to say anything. "I never expected to see you again, I mean, you're famous. Anyway, I-um, I have had a bit of a crush on, um, y-you since we were kids. And, um, I, um. . ." Her nerves were shot and she couldn't believe she was talking to Sam about her crush. She wanted to die from the irritation and indignity of the issue.

"It's okay, I'm not going anywhere." He pressed his lips to her forehead.

She took a deep breath hoping it would steady her rapid breathing. It didn't help. "You were my celebrity free pass." She felt her cheeks burn with mortification.

"Is that it?" He asked. "No illicit sex tapes? No criminal behaviour? No drunk driving convictions?"

"No, just the pass," she murmured.

"Paige, that's sweet." He paused and hugged her tighter. "I was expecting worse. The PR team will be on to it. For a moment, I thought there was going to be some sex tape of you going around that we'd have to get removed from the Internet. Which, by the way, is almost impossible."

She could hear the jovial tone in his voice, but knew he was covering up his incredulity at her behaviour. "It's not sweet."

"It is. And it's really nice and flattering of you to say that about me."

She stared at him, still unable to believe what he was saying. Surely, he was laughing at her stupidity. He was an actor, and actors acted.

In that moment, she decided to play along but she'd start to distance herself from him. It wasn't just the media, but also, she needed to protect her heart from being shattered into a million pieces when he returned to Hollywood. There was a reason he was her celebrity pass, and not just because he was good looking.

"Let me speak to my PR team and manage it. We'll turn it into a cute romantic story." He leaned over, lifted his phone from the coffee table and started typing. His thumbs moving quickly over the screen. And just like that, he'd managed the situation. And as much as she hated to admit it, she needed him because no one was going to listen to her. She had no pull or ability to impact the media... but he did.

She plonked herself back on the sofa, her head

fell back and she closed her eyes. The past couple of days had been the best she'd ever had. The sex. The seclusion. The shared secrets. It had been special but now it was over. She didn't know how she would return to her career, her family and her uninteresting life. It was like she was a snow globe that someone had shaken, the snow was falling around her, making her life very different from how it once had been.

"Everything will be fine," he reassured her, before kissing her nose.

His fingers massaged the stress from her neck. "We'll manage this. It's pretty tame compared to what I was expecting."

She rolled her eyes at him. "For you, not me." This was the worst moment in her life, and yet, he'd barely reacted over the news. Good acting? Or did he really not mind about the *pass*?

"I want to trust you, I do. But...knowing my parents will read this makes me want to crawl into a hole and never come out," she confessed in a low voice.

"I'm sorry you have to go through this." He held her closer to him. "But it's not that bad. It's kinda cute, and Megan will destroy him."

"Really?" Her breathing hitched, curious as to what Megan would do.

"Put it this way, I'm glad that Megan is on my side. I would not want to be on the receiving end of a phone call from her." He paused and gave her a cheeky grin. "There is a reason that she earns megabucks from me, and not just because she organises my life so well."

"She'll fix everything? She can do that?" She could hear the incredulity in her voice.

"For sure. She can handle worse, this will be easy for her," he said with a dismissive wave of his hand.

"In a few hours, Mike will wish he'd never done the interview or hurt you."

The cold tone in his voice made her look up, as concern spiked in her belly. "You're going to crush him?"

"For sure. No one hurts you, and gets away with it," he said.

She bit her lip. She was flattered that he was protecting her but was concerned about how far Megan would go. "I mean, I don't want...he's not going to lose his job or die or anything?"

He gave her a reassuring smile. "No, we'll put him in his place and remind him that you are an amazing woman who doesn't deserve to be treated like that. He'll wish he'd shut up in the first place and not gone to the media."

She didn't know whether to be relieved or not. "I

don't want him to be humiliated to a point he kills himself or something," she admitted. "I'm so angry at Mike, but I don't want something that bad to happen to him."

He pressed his lips to her forehead. "Nothing like that."

She relaxed into his arms, snuggling against his lean, hard body. "Thank you."

"You're welcome," he said. "Security will be here in fifteen minutes, wanna make out?" He gave her a cheeky grin.

As if she'd say no to that.

A FEW HOURS LATER, they were back in Melbourne in a five-star hotel, and Sam was surrounded by his team. Paige felt like an outsider and was bored. There was nothing to do, except watch TV. She needed to exercise, get outside.

Despite the cool air, the sun shone and Paige's heart lifted as she made her way outside with her skateboard. Dressed in her favourite jeans, sweater, and runners, she navigated the busy streets till she reached the Carlton Gardens. The stillness and beauty of the gardens always made her feel calm, and she loved the serenity of the garden beds, mani-cured lawns, and large trees. She skated along the paths, alone, enjoying this freedom to relax. She skated up to the Royal Exhibition Building and admired the large stately complex built in the nineteenth century.

She'd been gone an hour, and doubted she was missed. She continued along past the Melbourne Museum when she heard her name being called. Instinctively she turned, looking around. She turned back and gasped as a toddler ran out in front of her. She tried to swerve but her and her skateboard went flying, and she landed with a thump on the beautifully manicured lawn.

"Ow," she said, landing on her arm. With difficulty, she raised her head, and saw that the child had been collected by her mum.

"Are you okay?" A worried voice asked.

She felt like the breath had been punched out of her. Wiggling her toes and then her fingers, she was happy that no bones had broken with her fall, but she'd be bruised from the landing. Thankfully, she'd ended up on grass and not on cement. "I think so," she replied. Her head ached. She adjusted her glasses and said a prayer of thanks they hadn't broken or shattered into her eyes.

"Shall I call an ambulance?"

Paige lifted her gaze to the young woman seated beside her, holding a toddler, whose arms were flailing. The woman's eyes were filled with compassion and concern.

"I think I'm bruised, and so is my ego." She admitted in a low voice.

"I'm sorry about my son. He was running, but you didn't see him, your attention was diverted, or so it seemed."

"Muuummmmmmy." The little boy tried to extract himself from the protective arms of his mother.

She kissed his forehead. "Just a minute, we need to check on this lady."

Suddenly, there were a few people surrounding them. Paige only realised when the warmth of the sun was blocked, and the young woman's eyes opened wide with worry.

"Paige, what's it like being the girlfriend of Sam?"

"Did Sam mind that he's your celebrity pass?"

"Are you and Sam going to marry?"

"Did you have a fight? Why isn't he here?"

The young woman waved her arm in the air before shouting. "Leave her alone."

"You almost knocked a young child down. Are you upset about Sam leaving you?" And on and on, the questions were fired at her.

The young boy started to cry. "I'm so sorry," the young woman said as she moved away, getting away from the pack of media wolves surrounding them.

Paige was still on the grass, and she had no idea where her skateboard was. Not that she could skate away. Her body ached from the impact of the fall and she tugged her phone from her back pocket, with difficulty. With shaking fingers, she sent a message to Sam, his private details were listed in her phone as "Dad." "Need help. Hurt. Media." she typed to him. She sat up, her shoulders slumped and she closed her eyes, willing that the media would leave her. They didn't. They continued to take photos of her, as she sat there, her forehead resting on her bent knees, waiting to be rescued.

How stupid had she been?

She'd told Megan she was going downstairs to get a coffee. She'd lied and paid the price for her betrayal. Not thinking about the consequences of her actions, she'd winded herself, bruised the right side of her body, and botched things up…again.

No one was going to believe she was the girl-friend of Sam. She was too clumsy, and too normal. She should've been upfront and look at what had happened.

Suddenly Sam's security team burst through the throng of people circling her. Strong arms lifted her, and carried her away.

"You're trouble with a capital T." The security guard carried her with an ease that would impress a wrestler. In his strong arms, she allowed her body to sag with relief, and despite the media chasing them, she felt safe and protected. "We were watching you, and we'd scouted the area and it seemed safe. We go for a leak, and then you've had an accident and got the media on you."

"I'm so sorry," she said with honesty. Her lip warbled and she bit it to stop trembling. "I was bored, and needed to get out. I shouldn't have lied, sorry for the trouble."

"It's fine. We have a tracker on your phone, we've been watching you the whole time," he said depositing her in the large SUV with black tinted windows. "Jack's got your board, we'll leave in a minute."

She sagged against the leather softness of the backseat, and closed her eyes, blocking out the media as they badgered her through the dark glass. Using her hand, she covered her face to protect herself from the camera flashes. What a mess.

If this was how Sam lived his life, he could keep it.

She thought she'd been so clever to leave, but she'd forgotten the tracker that Megan had put on her mobile phone. Megan could read all her messages, and had access to her life.

Urgh, she groaned.

She hated all of this.

There was no privacy. Not only had she lost her "life" in this short time, but she'd lost her own self.

This was only a taste of what would come if she and Sam were together.

Not that he'd asked or that she expected anything beyond his time in Australia. But even if he wanted something long term with her, how could she do it? This was awful.

To have no privacy, not be able to go out in public without being accosted by the media, or fans. What a life. And that was not a good thing. This bubble-like existence where everyone watched you was not something she could get used to. She was hating it so far, and it had only been one week.

The car moved into the city traffic and away from the media. They had their story. It wouldn't be real, and she didn't care.

She knew she didn't belong in Sam's world. But when it was just the two of them, she forgot all about it. He was funny, smart, and sexy. The perfect guy for her, except he was a star, adored by millions of women.

"You okay?" the driver asked.

"Sore, but okay," she replied.

"A doctor is coming to the suite to check on you," he said.

Great! Not only had she snuck out, lied to Megan, but she'd been caught out in the worse way. It was going to be plastered on social media and night news. Sam was going to be livid.

That was the understatement of the year.

SAM WAS LIVID...AT himself. He was used to his life and being a celebrity, but Paige wasn't. How could he expect her to understand that sneaking out was a terrible idea, when he hadn't been there for her?

He swore under his breath.

Caught in his charity work, he hadn't thought about Paige. He should've included her, asked for her opinions instead of leaving her alone.

When she walked into the room at that moment with the security guards, her face was ashen white, and his stomach plummeted with remorse. This was *his* fault.

"Everyone, out," he pointed to the door. In seconds, it was just him and Paige.

"I'm so sorry," she said, and he could see she was visibly distraught about the incident.

"I'm the one who's sorry, not you. I should've been there for you," he tugged her close and hugged her hard.

"You're not angry at me?" Her voice was filled with confusion, mixed with remorse.

He lifted his head and looked at her. "No. I'm angry at myself, not you."

"B-but, after what I did?" Her lip was trembling, and he could see she was upset from the ordeal.

Taking her hand, he walked her to the sofa, and they sat opposite each other, but he held her hands in his. "I should've warned you. And I should've remembered you were here."

"I lied—" she interrupted him.

"I don't care about that. Are you hurt? The doctor will be here soon," he said before pressing his lips against hers. "I was worried about you. Tell me what happened?" A heavy sense of responsibility weighed heavily on his shoulders. He wasn't going to let her down, again.

She rubbed her eyes. "A toddler ran in front of me, I swerved but ended up on the grass—"

"Did you knock your head? I hope you don't have a concussion?" His fingers gently touched her forehead and then ran along her hairline, looking for a lump.

He sighed a breath of relief when he didn't feel or see one.

"No, but I was winded." Her shoulders slumped with the admittance. "The toddler's mum checked on me but then we were surrounded by the media. She panicked and then she left. I would've done the same. It was awful. And I feel so bad for her."

His fingers caressed her pulse point and he could feel the erratic beat of her heart. She was in shock. "She's fine, but I need to make sure you're okay. Let the doctor check you. Okay?"

She gave him a weak smile. "Fine."

He held her close, relieved she was okay, not just from the fall but from the reporters who'd hounded her. Hounded her at the worst time. As she was injured, they'd swarmed over her, not bothering to check if she was hurt. His fist clenched with anger.

There was a knock at the door, interrupting his thoughts. "Yes?" he called out.

The door to the suite opened, and Megan walked in. "The doctor is here."

A young man wearing a suit followed Megan. He looked too handsome, and not haggard enough to be a doctor, in his opinion, and he lifted an eyebrow before shooting a questioning look at Megan.

"He's legit," she announced. "As if?" She rolled her eyes.

He smothered a chuckle. He was always on guard, but he knew Megan would never let him down. Of course, she would ensure the doctor was not some wanna-be actor pretending to get close to him.

He ran his fingers through his hair. There were times he was really sick of this industry, and everything that went with it.

The doctor was simply a good-looking man, that was it. He caught Megan looking at the man, who introduced himself as Dr Love.

Paige chuckled with astonishment. "Are you making that up to make me feel better?"

"Not at all," the young man said, handing her a business card.

"Dr Julian Love," she read out with a smile.

He shuffled a few centimetres away from Paige, and watched the interaction between her and Dr Love.

An unfamiliar shot of jealousy stabbed at his belly, as he noticed Paige's smile. That smile was thanks to Dr Love, not him. Crap.

"I get asked that all the time," the man said. He sat next to Paige, and placed his bag on the floor. Using a stethoscope, he checked her heartbeat and breathing. "My family emigrated to Australia from Poland in the 1930s, before the war. They learnt English on the boat over, but when they registered their name, the Australian official struggled with their accent and the pronunciation of the name Lozowski." The man then ran his fingers over Paige's arms and forehead. "They recorded the family name as Love, and my grandparents were happy to have anglicised their name. They didn't realise, at the time, what Love was. But when they did, they liked it and kept the new name."

Paige chuckled, and he could see the skin on her face was looking much better, and she'd lost that shocked look.

Obviously, Dr Love was good at making his patients feel at ease. And so were other women in the near vicinity. His eyes almost popped out of his sockets when he saw Megan, his assistant…smiling. Her focus was on the young man, and he could see she was totally transfixed by him. Astonishing. He'd never seen her interested in any guy. And yet here she was with a stupid grin on her face, watching Dr Love.

"We have a tradition in our family that first-born sons are called Julian." The doctor chatted while checking her blood pressure.

"You have a lot of Julian Loves in your family?" Paige asked, her lips twitched in a smile.

"Surprisingly no. I am surrounded by three

sisters, and girl cousins. Apart from my Dad, I'm the only boy in the family."

"That couldn't be easy. I'm one of four girls, so I understand what it's like," she said with a reassuring nod. "My Dad never minded, but I'm sure it wasn't easy when we were all teenage girls. He spent much time in his office."

"I hated being the only boy when I was younger, but then in my teens, I was surrounded by my sister's friends." He gave Paige a *you know what I mean* wink.

"Oh, you," Paige chuckled, giving his arm a friendly punch. "Such a bloke."

Sam's stomach curdled with annoyance as he watched the friendly banter between Paige and the doctor, and he had an uncharacteristic urge to punch the man's handsome face. Stupid. The doctor wasn't flirting; they were chatting, and he was behaving like a jealous teen. He ran his fingers through his hair, unable to believe how idiotic he was feeling. This trip to Melbourne was becoming very different from what he'd been expecting.

"Now tell me, Paige, when you fell, did you lose consciousness?"

"No."

"Did you have blurred vision?"

"No."

And on he went, asking questions.

Feeling superfluous and also needing to get away, he stood and stalked to the kitchen to make himself a strong coffee. He wasn't feeling friendly. He wanted to hoist Paige over his shoulder and take her to his bedroom. He wanted to be with her. Seeing her smile and chuckle with another man, even if it was a doctor, was like a red-hot poker being shoved between his ribs.

He'd never been jealous before and had no idea how to manage the annoyance zipping up and down his back.

He decided to do what he did best…act. Act like everything was fine, like he didn't mind another man was making *his* Paige smile.

He swallowed an expletive and stalked back into the room, coffee in hand. Then he stopped. Megan stood in exactly the same position that she had been for the past few minutes. Leaning against the wall, arms crossed over her chest, her focus was on…the doctor.

Megan was watching the doctor, intently. Instead of answering messages on her phone and doing a million things at once like she always did, Dr Love had diverted her attention.

Crap.

Not only was Paige transfixed with him, but it

seemed his assistant was, too. No way. He was going to get rid of the doctor as soon as he could.

Sidling next to Megan he said, "I need you to finalise everything for my charity date?"

Not even looking at him, she said, "It's all done."

Frustration ate into his belly, and he stepped in front of her, blocking her view of Dr Love and Paige. "Confirm it for me," he snapped.

Her eyes widened, not expecting the harsh tone of his voice. "It's conf—" And then she stopped, realising he wanted her to leave. "Sure, I'm on to it." Walking out of the room, she strode to the spare room she was using as her office and slammed the door behind her.

Sam felt like a heel, but he needed to be Megan's top priority. He had paid her an exorbitant wage not only because she was worth it, but he expected her to be on call for *him*, 24/7.

He cracked his knuckles and drew in a steady breath before he walked over to Paige.

"So, doc, everything okay?" he asked before seating himself next to Paige.

"I think so. She seems bruised and sore, from the fall but it doesn't seem that she's had a concussion or any broken bones," the man said.

"I told you," Paige said in a tell-tale voice.

Sam touched her nose with his finger. "It's better to be careful."

Dr Love wrote a note and handed it to Paige. "I've suggested a bruise cream for your arm and some over-the-counter medication for pain relief." He paused. "I'll come and check on you tomorrow but if you start vomiting or start feeling dizzy you must go to a hospital emergency."

Paige nodded. "Thanks Julian, I'm sure I'll be fine."

"I'll check on her during the night and make sure she's okay," he said, placing his arm around her shoulders, ignoring Paige's eyes opening wide with surprise.

He stood and held out his hand. "Thank you, Doctor, for coming on such short notice."

Dr Love shook his hand. "My surgery is nearby so the hotel often calls me for help with their patients." He turned to Paige. "See you tomorrow." He gathered his instruments, and notebook, methodically placing them in his briefcase.

He shook Paige's hand and then left.

"Did you have to act all protective and caveman like?" she glared at him, the skin between her eyes was deeply creased. "Honestly," she said with a roll of her eyes. She stood. "I'm going to lie down. Would you mind if one of your staff got me the items I need?" She thrust the piece of paper from the doctor at him.

And before he could answer, she'd stalked off and slammed the door behind her.

Two angry women. Megan. Paige. Two slammed doors.

He rubbed his hands over his eyes

He could use some advice on how to handle women now. First time ever.

CHAPTER 13

*P*aige knew she was being unfairly harsh with Sam, but she couldn't help the mixed feelings she was experiencing. Sam had been overprotective, which was ridiculous of him. Julian was a doctor and had been totally professional over the past half hour. There was nothing inappropriate in Julian's manner, yet Sam's tone of voice, and the way he sat between the two of them came across as caveman like. Goodness sakes.

She lay on the bed and closed her eyes thinking about the day.

This goldfish bowl existence was not for her, and as much as she was going to miss Sam when he returned to LA, she knew she didn't fit into his world. And even if she tried, what would she do all day? It wasn't like she could just get a job in her field.

It was a different country with different laws and different processes.

She let out a long, frustrated breath.

She was too sensible and knew that she only had a few more days with Sam, and he still had to spend time with his parents and go on *the date*.

The date. She scratched her chin and wondered who had been lucky enough to win Sam's competition. Where would they go? What would they do?

A knock on the door made her realise that she'd fallen into a light sleep, thinking about Sam.

"It's just me," Megan said walking in with a tray. "I've got pain relief, and I also made you a cup of coffee with the chocolate cookies you love."

Paige sat up. "You're a gem, thanks," she said, watching the other woman place the tray beside her. "You got the bruise cream for me," she exclaimed, seeing the tube on the tray.

Megan nodded. "Anything else you need?"

Paige swallowed hard, knowing she owed Megan an apology. "I'm sorry for lying to you. That was not cool, I shouldn't have done it."

"No, you shouldn't have," Megan snapped at her. "At your apartment, I told you that I was in charge. Don't ever go off like that again. You compromised your own security, plus you were injured."

Her head hung in shame as Megan lectured her,

making her feel like a teen being reprimanded. "I'm sorry."

Megan crossed her arms over her chest. "You may be Sam's friend, lover, whatever." She gave her a tight smile. "In a week he'll be gone and we'll be back home. You may think that this…"—she searched for the right word with a roll of her eyes—"Friendship is going to last, but it won't. You two have history, but Sam is one of Hollywood's most popular actors. He's on the cover of magazines. He's a star."

"I know that," she said with an annoyed press of her lips. She hated that Megan treated her like an idiot. Of course, she knew that.

"I'm reminding you that Sam is returning to LA soon *without you*," she continued, her shoulders squared and her stance rigid.

"Just because he's taking you to meet his parents doesn't mean there is some *happily ever after*." She paused. "I felt that as his *teen friend*, you should go with him, and it suited his image. I just don't want you getting the wrong idea."

Ignoring the bruised pain in her arms and all down the side of her body where she'd fallen, she swung her legs around, then hopped off the bed and stood directly in front of Sam's PA. She was sick of being treated like she was stupid. Standing firm, she placed her hands on her hips. "I'm twenty-nine not nineteen, and my relationship with Sam is actually none of your business." She pressed her lips together. "I know who Sam is, and I don't need you reminding me of *my place*. I know exactly how things are. Thank you for the medication, but you can leave now."

Megan's eyes blazed with exasperation and surprise. "Fine," she said before turning on her heel and walking out of the room in her stilettos.

The confidence in her body collapsed out of her, and she sat on the side of the bed. The practical Paige knew everything that Megan has said was right. She and Sam were having an affair, a fling, and soon it would be over. But even knowing it, she was dreading the day she'd have to say goodbye to him.

He was her friend, he was her lover, he was special to her.

She doubted that he thought of her as more than a good friend and lover. But as soon as he returned to his life in LA, he'd forget all about her.

Maybe she'd get an occasional message? She shrugged. But after he was back acting and then promoting his movies, he'd be too busy to think about her.

She had a week. A week to be with him and enjoy his company, and also his lovemaking. He was right. They were fantastic together. She'd never had so many orgasms before, and she couldn't get enough of him.

She loved touching him, pleasuring him, kissing him.

Stupid to stay in the room, moping like a child. She was determined to be with him till the moment she and he parted.

He was her dream come true. The guy she'd spent years fantasising about. And she had him. It might be a short time, but she'd be a fool not to make the most of it.

With determination, she leaned over, sipped her coffee, ate the cookies, and took two tablets of pain relief. Then she stood and made her way out of the room, determined to speak to Sam.

THE FOLLOWING few days passed in a haze of media interviews, interviews as part of Sam's mentoring program and of course, amazing sex.

Whether it was late at night or a quickie in his room, they were drawn to each other, seeking each other out, wanting that moment when they became one. Her body hummed with pleasure and anticipation of being with him.

And in front of his staff and others, she'd let her guard down, touching him, caressing his face and brushing her lips against his. The need to touch him and let him know how much she wanted him was so strong that she couldn't fight it.

The media loved it and ran many articles about them, speculating about the longevity of their relationship.

And then it was time for them to be apart, so Sam could go on *the date*.

He'd raised four million dollars for his personal charity. In LA, he subsidised two schools catering to those students who couldn't afford tuition to work in the arts industry. Whether it was camera work, acting or makeup, a number of talented young people had been able to find work thanks to Sam's generosity in providing them free education.

Lying naked in bed together, Sam's fingers ran along her shoulder and down her arm. "I'm flying to Queensland tomorrow to meet *my date*." He pressed his lips against hers. "I want you to come with me."

"But Megan said no, I was to stay here," she said with a sigh. She really wanted to be with Sam, every moment she could and was disappointed to have missed out.

"Megan works for me, and I have decided you're coming with me." His mouth nuzzled her breasts before his tongue licked her nipple to a hard pebble.

"I don't want to cause any issues," she tried to say,

but her mouth became dry as Sam started to kiss her neck while his hands massaged her breasts. "I can't talk when you do that for me."

"I want you, now," he said, his voice husky and needy.

Their coupling was swift, fast, and hard.

"I can't get enough of you," he whispered in her ear. "I want you with a need that is so strong. I've never felt like this before."

She shivered in reply. It was the same for her. She kissed him in return because there were no words. What could she say? *Take me to LA with you*? She didn't want that. She wanted him to stay here in Australia with her. But that couldn't happen. He was a star. His life was over there.

She put her arms around him and held him tight, unable to say the words, because she didn't want to hear the answer.

She just had to enjoy this time before he was gone.

Much later, snuggled up against him, she asked, "Can you tell me about your date now?"

"I recorded the announcement today and it will be going out tonight on social media. The winner, who you know is from England, flies into Queensland tomorrow morning."

"She'll be tired after the long flight to Australia,"

she said, drowsy from hours of lovemaking and time in bed with Sam.

"She is actually a he," he said in a very straight, sincere voice.

She stilled and then sat up. "What do you mean?"

He gave her a teasing smile. "A guy won the competition, not a woman."

"Really?" She smiled, curious as to who he was.

"Yes," he cleared his throat. "Oliver is gay, and um, I'm his favourite actor."

"O-kay," she said slowly. "And he wants a date with you, even though you're not gay."

"Yep," he said.

"I didn't think about men entering the competition, no wonder you've been laughing at me, every time I refer to the winner as a she."

"I wanted to tell you, but I couldn't. I'm sorry," he said before pressing his lips against her forehead.

"Where are you going?"

"To Cairns." He mentioned a popular tourist city in Far North Queensland. "His dream date was to see the Daintree Rainforest."

"It's beautiful there. What a great choice," she clapped her hands together. "You'll have the most amazing time together."

"Honestly, I would prefer to be with you," he

brushed his lips against hers. "But I'm excited to be on a date that's more than a candlelit dinner."

"We'll be flying to Cairns in the morning, meet Oliver, and then drive up to a resort about an hour and a half north of Cairns. We'll have dinner with Oliver, and the following day we take a cruise along the Daintree River, have a picnic lunch, and then we go ziplining."

"That sounds amazing," she said.

"We should have time after to visit the Wildlife Habitat so Oliver can see some native Australian animals," he said.

"What a date, Megan has been efficient as usual," she said. Megan may not be her favourite person, especially after the recent run-in, but she had to admit Megan was the type of assistant anyone would want.

She snuggled next to him, secretly wishing it was her going ziplining with Sam but said nothing. "You're going to have the best date."

"If you'd won, where would you have chosen to go?" His fingers ran through her hair.

She blushed, remembering how she'd fantasised about having a date with Sam all those weeks ago. "Um," she cleared her throat. "I would have suggested snorkelling on the Barrier Reef."

"That's a good choice, too," he said. "Come on,

time for sleep, we have an early start tomorrow morning." He pressed his lips against her hair.

She fell asleep in his arms, dreaming about her and Sam back at the lake house, when it was just the two of them.

THE FLIGHT UP north was uneventful, and Sam used his time to read the script for the movie he was soon to start. Another romantic comedy. The female lead was known to him. Although super popular with the fans, she could be difficult and demanding on set, and Sam hoped it didn't cause too many problems with filming.

They'd met Oliver, and he was the same age as him, similar in height and build. The guy was friendly, despite his nerves, and excited to meet his favourite star.

Sam had smiled warmly for photos, selfies and everything that was required, before they all headed up north to the resort.

He'd barely had any time with Paige alone, and even though he expected it, he was already missing her.

She'd stayed out of the limelight except to welcome Oliver and ask about his flight over.

He and Oliver had enjoyed a casual dinner of steak and beer together, and the conversation flowed easily. Oliver was a great "date," and the type of guy he'd be friends with. In fact, Oliver reminded him of Harry, his best mate in LA.

In his room, he found Paige asleep in their bed. A check at the time showed how late it was. He watched her while she slept, and his heart warmed, thinking about their time together. Leaning over he brushed his lips across hers, but she barely stirred in her sleep. Not wanting to wake her, he undressed quickly and slid in the sheets beside her.

THE FOLLOWING day they cruised down the river, enjoying the beauty of the natural rainforest. Their guide was knowledgeable and also interesting. It was only he and Oliver on the cruise, and then after a quick picnic of mouth-watering sandwiches and fruit, they headed up to the ziplining.

He'd included Paige and Megan in the ziplining. Although his focus was on Oliver, he didn't want them to miss out.

After being harnessed, wearing helmets, and more photos, he zipped down, through the rainforest where he was treated to aerial views of the rainforest and Great Barrier Reef.

For a moment, he was Sam. Not Sam the star, but Sam, a guy who was enjoying time away from the pressures of his busy career. He forgot about everything and really allowed himself to have fun. He was truly relaxed and laughing. It wasn't forced, and he wasn't acting.

"This is brilliant," Oliver called out to him in his clipped English accent, as they zipped down. "Did you see the views?"

"Yes." He called out, his voice filled with joy.

"Tomorrow, I'm going snorkelling on the Barrier Reef," Oliver said.

"You should, you can't travel all the way here and not see it."

"I'm so glad I was chosen. I'm having the time of my life," Oliver called out, as they zipped down.

Me too, he thought. This was what he was missing from his life in LA, the fun of being with a friend. He really only had Harry. And soon Harry would be leaving to live overseas. He didn't blame him. He wouldn't want to stay in LA if his wife cheated on him. What a mess.

Once they reached the base, they removed their harnesses and helmets and enjoyed an afternoon tea of fruit, cake, and coffee and tea. Despite it being winter, the day was warm and sunny, so typical of the tropical location of Northern Queensland.

Whilst Oliver chatted with Megan, he used the time to speak with Paige. "Did you enjoy that?"

She gave him a grin that melted his insides. "Thanks for bringing me along. That was the best fun I've had."

"You're welcome." He'd ensured Paige and Megan had been able to enjoy the zipline too, and he was pleased Paige was having a good day. She hadn't encroached on his time with Oliver, and had melted into the background.

"We're going to the zoo soon, and then we return to Melbourne. It will be a late night," he said. Back to his busy schedule.

"Sure. It's a shame we can't stay here longer. It's so beautiful here," she said.

He took a moment to admire her long legs. She was wearing a T-shirt that had a logo of a popular 70s TV show and shorts. Her hair was tied back in a ponytail and messy after being squashed by the helmet. Her face was free of makeup, and her skin glowed with vitality and happiness. To him, she was stunning. Even more beautiful than any of the women he'd had accompany him along the red carpet over the years.

He was going to miss her. Paige was very different from the women he usually met and spent time with. She was down to earth, smart, and funny.

Because of their shared history, she was relaxed around him. They had fun together. And also, she was amazing in bed. Their connection was unlike anything he'd ever experienced. She was special. And soon, he'd have to leave her behind. A thump of pain hit him in the belly, thinking about being alone again. He'd enjoyed this time with her more than he'd expected to. How boring life would be back in LA, without Paige and without Harry.

"You look like you're a million miles away," Paige interrupted his thoughts.

He pushed them aside and pretended he was okay. "Just thinking. Are you ready to go?"

At the zoo, they fed the animals, learnt about their native habitats, and had the obligatory photo holding a koala.

He even noticed that Megan had organised one for herself, and he could see she loved every moment. Dressed casually, she looked more relaxed and happy. He made his way to her. "I'm glad you had a photo, too."

Megan gave him an unexpected grin. "Thought you owed me one after I've babysat your girlfriend for you."

His lips pressed against each other, and his fists clenched. "You work for me, and you do an excellent job, but you will not speak badly of Paige. Got it?"

Her eyes widened in surprise. "Yeah, sure, sorry."

"I'm glad you had your photo taken, you deserve it, but helping Paige is part of the job description."

"Sure, Sam. And thanks for zipline, I really enjoyed it."

"You're welcome."

"We've got half an hour before we need to head back to the airport," she said with her usual efficient manner.

"I'm staying here tonight—"

She interrupted him. "A private jet is waiting to return us to Melbourne."

"Fix it, so we leave in a day's time." He was relaxed, and wasn't ready to return to his celebrity life. He needed, but also wanted, some more time away.

She bit her lip. "But—"

"After my date with Oliver ends, Paige and I are staying here tomorrow and going back the day after. Please organise. I just. . .I need some time off, okay?"

Her face softened. "Sure. Whatever you want."

He then told her of his plans and what needed to be done.

With her usual organised efficiency, she typed it all in her phone. "I'm on to it."

"Thanks," he said, before taking some deep breaths. He'd just changed his schedule which would impact his parents and his social media calendar. He didn't care. He'd call his parents tonight and apologise and see them another time.

For the first time in ten years, he was being selfish. He was doing what he wanted, and not what was expected of him.

He was going to spend time with Paige.

CHAPTER 14

The following morning after breakfast, Sam, Paige, and his security headed out on a boat to the Great Barrier Reef.

The day was warm, typical of the tropical north, and Sam was feeling energised and happy.

Megan had given him a rundown of his itinerary while he pumped weights early that morning, then asked to be excused so she could sleep. He'd waved her off, telling her to spend the day in bed ignoring the twinge of guilt in his belly. Megan had stayed up late to rework his schedule, and she deserved a day of Netflix in bed. He'd also instructed her to utilise the benefits of the spa, and enjoy whichever treatments she wanted and to add it to his tab.

"Sure, it will be my pleasure to spend your

money," she said with a cheeky wink, before returning to her room.

The boat was large and could easily accommodate twenty extra people, but without crowds and fans asking for a selfie, Sam could actually relax. Being in the public eye meant that he never relaxed fully, always aware that someone was watching him. Watching him to report gossip to the media.

But here, they were alone. No prying eyes and no need to worry about a rogue reporter snapping a photo of him. Peaceful.

He took a deep breath and stared out into the blue waters. Allowing his brain to shut down, he enjoyed the warmth of the sun, the salty taste of the sea spray and the quietness.

Paige came and wrapped her arms around him. "We'll be there in about an hour. Thank you for organising this, I can't believe we're having a whole day together."

"I needed it," he said, which he meant on two levels, needing time alone and needing time with her.

"The guys"—Her head jerked towards the security men—"are pretty excited to be spending the day out at the Reef. That's a good perk of looking after a celeb." She chuckled at her own joke. "You're lost in your thoughts. You have that faraway look in your eyes."

He kissed her nose. "I don't get much time to relax. It's pretty unusual for me to have a day off like this."

"I know. And thanks for organising a date with me. I'm… I'm really excited," she confessed with a voice bursting with enthusiasm. "Thanks for my dream date. I may not have won your competition, but these past couple of weeks have been magic."

He nodded in agreement. "We'll have a couple of hours snorkelling before we have lunch on the boat, and then head back." He paused. "We're flying back to Melbourne tonight, and then seeing my parents tomorrow."

"I hope your parents weren't too disappointed about the date change," she said with sincerity.

"They understand my life all too well," he said in a low voice. He'd spoken to them last night and been open and upfront about needing some quiet time before he returned to LA. They were his parents, his family, his support. They understood.

Paige in her usual casual garb was wearing a green bikini top together with cropped denim jeans, and a large hat protected her face from the sun. His finger traced the skin along her shoulder blades. "I hope you put sunscreen on. I don't want you to burn." He nibbled her ear. "I could massage some cream on you now."

She grinned. "That sounds like a fine idea," she said taking his hands and tugging him down towards the cabins below deck.

* * *

IF PAIGE HAD to list the top happy moments in her life, this would be one of them. It was comparable with her graduating and her nephew hugging her and giving her squishy kisses.

But this was truly special.

In the warm, blue waters, she and Sam were snorkelling and looking at the magnificence of the Great Barrier Reef. It was something she'd always wanted to do, but either never had the time or the money to do so.

It felt like they were the only people around. There were no other boats, and apart from the crew and security, she and Sam were alone, free to be themselves.

They held hands, faces in the water, slowly kicking their feet as they admired the stunning beauty of natural corals.

She gasped seeing her first clownfish. *Nemo*. She couldn't tell Sam of her excitement because of her mask and snorkel, but he saw the fish too and gave her a thumbs-up.

They drifted around, the flippers on their feet made it easy to float on the water and admire the stunning beauty. They saw hundreds of fish and sea turtles.

From the pocket of his board shorts, Sam retrieved an underwater camera and snapped photos of the fish, coral and…her.

Exhausted after an amazing time in the water, they swam back to the boat and dried themselves.

"Did you swim?" Sam asked Jack, one of the security guards.

"Yeah, thanks. We took it in turns. One of us swam while the other watched out." He paused. "That was great, thanks man."

Paige could see genuine joy in the security man's face, and it made her realise the loyalty they had for Sam.

The staff then served a buffet of salads, cold chicken, and quiche, followed by cake and fruit. She and Sam sat with the security guards, and enjoyed the lunch provided to them. Paige ate a lot since she was famished after the long swim.

She noticed that neither of the men drank alcohol, and even though their slouched posture in the seats had them relaxed, their eyes betrayed them.

They still looked out, especially with the sounds of other boats nearby. And Jack kept his gaze on the staff.

No wonder Sam thought she was the leak to the newspapers. His staff were not just loyal, but they were constantly ensuring he was safe.

The walk on the red carpet had been two weeks ago, but it felt like a lifetime. So much had happened since.

After lunch, the staff cleaned up, and then it was just the two of them.

Sam took her hands in his and tugged her towards him, so they ended up seated face to face on one of the comfortable sofas.

"We'll be back at the resort in an hour, and then you need to pack, so we can drive to the airport," he said.

Her heart sank. This was it. This was the goodbye speech. Even though she knew it was coming, her heart thumped hard with dismay against her chest.

"I'm spending the day with my parents tomorrow, and I'd rather you didn't come. I don't get enough time with them, and I just want to be with them," he told her with honesty.

"I get that. And also, I don't want to give them false hopes about us," she said with uncertainty.

"They won't. They know you and I have been a

set-up from the beginning," he admitted, his gaze not meeting hers.

"Um, yes, of course," she mumbled. How stupid of her to think otherwise. "I guess this is the time that we say goodbye and that this has been great. Right?"

His finger trailed down the side of her face. "It's been more than that for me. Being with you has been amazing. You're kind, caring, and fun to be with."

"Thank you. But I get it. I'm too much *like* your parents. I'm an everyday kind of gal. You and I both know that I won't fit into your world of red carpets, parties, and social media." She took a steadying breath, but her voice still shook. "Even with a stylist, I don't fit in and to be honest, I don't want to. If you weren't such a star, things might be different. But you have this amazing career. You are idolised by millions of women, and I don't think I could handle the pressure of being with you. I'd be scrutinised in everything I did. And then it would reflect badly on you."

"Hearing you say that hurts my heart," he said in a quiet voice. "I sound like a tosser."

"You're not. You're an Australian actor who's made it big in Hollywood. It's the stuff of dreams. You're living a life that so few get a chance to, and you did that. Through your hard work." She paused.

"You should be proud of your achievements. And you've given back to the community, helping teens realise their dream. This is you, this is your life. Mine is here in Australia. Our paths have crossed and for a short time, it's been incredible. But you need to return to your world, and I need to return to mine."

"Everything you say is right and honest. But it's more than that for me," he said. "I can't ask you to leave your career and family, they mean everything to you. But I've seen the damage show biz can do to a relationship, and I don't want that for you and us."

He kissed the knuckles on her left hand. "I work in an industry that can be difficult and demanding. My parents' marriage was strained, and look at Harry and Tasha." He shook his head with disappointment. "I'm not taking that risk. Especially with you." He cleared his throat. "I'm about to work on a new movie, a rom-com where the heroine returns to her hometown, and we're shooting all the outdoor scenes in Colorado. It's beautiful there, but what it means is that I'll be away from LA during that time."

"I know. And that's your career. You go where the work is," she said with a despondent sigh. "Even if I followed you to LA, we'd be separated a lot, and when you compound that with the intense scrutiny and media pressure, I think we'll have issues. While you've been here, it's like we're in a bubble. Megan has ensured we had privacy, and it's been amazing having this time with you. It's been like a vacation romance."

He nodded and didn't say anything, but she could see the pain in his eyes.

"I just want to say, that um, this is really hard for me to say," she took a deep breath and placed her shaking hands in her lap. "I've fallen in love with *you*. You. Not the star, but the man that is you. You're clever, considerate and...great in bed." She whispered "great in bed" to him. "But even though I'm in love with you, I don't believe love conquers all." She made quotation marks in the air. "Look at the mistakes I've made." She threw her hands in the air for emphasis. "I'm clumsy, I'm a skater, I'm an everyday-ish girl." Her shoulders slumped with disappointment and she returned her hands to her lap. "I'm not the right person for you."

"You're wrong," he said. "You are the right person for me, but I don't know if I'm the right person for *you*."

His fingers smoothed away the surprised lines on her forehead. "I don't know what you mean," she said with a disbelieving voice.

"You're smart and caring, and you should be around the people who make you happy. You are surrounded by a family who love and need you. And you need them as much as they need you," he said with an assertive voice, his shoulders straight, filled with belief and confidence in what he was saying to her. "You told me that you love me, and I wish I could say the same to you." His face fell with sadness and confusion. "But honestly, I don't know. I've never been in love. I don't even know if I'm capable of being in love. My life is about acting, and pretending emotions. Almost everything I do is an act."

Her breath caught in her throat. "You were pretending with me?" Her chest tightened painfully at the thought.

"No, my beautiful Paige. Everything with *you* was real," he said. "But my life..." He ran his fingers through his hair, as he searched for the right words. "Until I came to Australia, I thought everything was great. But then I reconnected with you and heard of Harry's imminent divorce, and it's made me question all my beliefs."

He stopped. "I wish I could say I love you, but what I can say is that you mean the world to me. I love your outlook on life. I love your love for your family. I love your intelligence. I love that you see the real me. I love that when I wake up in the morning, you are by my side."

She stared at him, unsure of what to say. She knew he meant every word, every praise he'd uttered. This was from Sam, her lover, not Sam the star. They'd both bared their souls to each other, but neither had made concessions for the other. It was that they'd each recognised the barriers between them but not found a way to get around them.

Perhaps what she felt wasn't love? She felt raw and exposed by having told him of her feelings. Especially since he didn't feel the same way.

She was special to him, just not special enough.

Surprisingly, the realisation didn't upset her as much as she thought it would. She was a realist, after all.

Besides, what did she expect? That a Hollywood star would stop doing movies and settle down in Australia? As if?

Her limbs were numb and heavy. Nothing could be the same again. Because she'd resigned herself to the fact that even *if* he had declared his undying love for her, she wasn't sure she could follow him to LA. What would she do? The separation, when he worked, would be a massive wedge between them. She'd be bored and lonely. Her insecurities could not be brushed away. What could she say, *don't leave me, I'm lonely*? How pathetic would that be?

She needed to push aside her feelings, and focus

on what was real and tangible. Sam was her friend, and they'd had the most amazing time together over the past couple of weeks. Her dreams had come true. But her reality was an everyday guy, not him.

This time she'd find someone who she was more compatible, and not choose someone just because he was tall. The right guy was out there, she just needed to find him. At least this time with Sam had shown her how great things could be with the right guy.

"I love you and always will," she said in a soft voice. "You've shown me that I don't have to settle for second best like I did with Mike. Being with you has been wonderful but now you need to return to LA while I return to suburbia." She sighed with resignation. "If we were right for each other, we'd be able to make this work. We haven't been able to, which says a lot. Don't worry, I'm not going to make a scene or get upset."

"I know you'd never do that. Thank you for making my life so happy while I was here. I will treasure our time together." He brushed his lips against hers. "You deserve better than me."

Her throat clogged and she couldn't swallow. "Don't say that." She placed her hand on his chest and could feel the heavy thump of his beating heart.

"I do mean it," he said with a firm voice. "You deserve to be with a man who'll cook with you, wash dogs with you, and make you tea when you're sick. All you'll get from me is social media pressure, loneliness and weeks on your own. You deserve better than that."

She nodded but couldn't speak. Her mouth was dry and her heart was close to bursting with self-pity.

The time to part was now.

Goodbye Sam.

CHAPTER 15

*S*am walked into his empty home up in the hills of LA and looked around. Everything was the same as it had been when he'd left for Australia over three weeks ago. His housekeeper had ensured everything was spotless, and he knew without checking that the fridge was full of healthy snacks, dinner, and his favourite cold-pressed juice.

He walked to the balcony, opened the door and looked at the sprawling mass of lights that was LA. He should be happy.

His latest movie was doing brilliantly, and his agent was being inundated with movie roles. But he was tired, and not just from the long flight, but his whole body felt exhausted from leaving his parents behind, and also Paige.

He didn't want to say her name or even think it.

But he still tortured himself each day scrolling through the photos on his phone of them. Had he really taken that many of them together? In such a short time, he'd filled his phone with selfies of them grinning. His favourite photo was taken on his date with Oliver. The staff were helping her with her harness for the zipline and she'd turned and smiled at him. He loved the candid nature of the photo, and the genuine warmth in her smile.

He turned his phone off, unable to look at her and not feel regret.

He'd handled her confession badly, but at least he'd been honest. Well, that's what he told himself. Really, he should've been more frank and upfront with her.

He grabbed a beer from the fridge and collapsed on the sofa, looking at the outside view.

Why wasn't he happy?

He should be but he wasn't.

A ping on his phone made him turn it on, and he read the email from Megan reminding him of his commitments over the next few days.

After taking a long sip from his beer, he tossed the phone aside, shucked his shoes and stretched his legs out.

He was tired, jet-lagged and dejected.

Megan's email could wait.

His self-reflection couldn't.

As he drained the last of his beer, his phone rang. Reluctantly he lifted his cell expecting it to be Megan but a smile stretched across his lips when he saw it was Harry calling him. "How are you, man?"

"Been better," Harry said, his voice full of self-pity. "How was the vacation?"

Sam chuckled at Harry's quip. "Good."

"You sound as pathetic as me," Harry replied. "I'm outside, buzz me in."

Within minutes, they were seated next to each other, each with a cold bottle of beer, looking out at the view.

They clinked bottle necks. "Cheers," he said at the same time as Harry toasted, "To Tasha getting crabs."

Pfft. "You're lucky my mouth wasn't full of beer, or you'd be wearing it."

"At least you haven't been down on my wife, sorry, soon-to-be ex-wife," Harry said, his voice filled with remorse. "Bad enough to find some guy's head between my wife's legs, but did it have to be Tom?" He looked up at the ceiling and swore. "Seriously, if I find out you screwed her, I'll punch you in the face." Harry lifted his arm, fist clenched.

Sam raised his hands defensively. "Easy man, you know I'd never do that to you."

Harry lowered his arm. His shoulders slumped with dejection. "Well, I didn't expect Tom to, either." He took a long sip of his beer. "We go to basketball together. Now I need a new friend. I think I'm going to get a dog. A dog won't let me down. Besides, I've always wanted a dog. Tasha hates dogs."

"I'm really sorry, man," Sam said, his heart full of pain and sorrow for his friend. He took a moment to take in the deep lines around his eyes and mouth, and dark shadows under his eyes. "You haven't slept much lately, have you?"

"Nope." He drained his beer, then stood and got another. "I've been drinking too much beer, eating pizza and watching sports. I even watched that Australian football that you like. I had no idea of the rules, but it passed the time."

Sam's stomach clenched with concern. "I'm worried about you."

"I'm the laughing stock at my work, and in LA." He popped the cap off the beer, stalked over and flopped on the sofa. "Apparently it's my fault that Tasha has been having affairs."

"Don't listen to the gossip." Sam waved his hand in the air.

"This town stinks." Harry sipped his beer.

"I've put on a few pounds, thanks to the beer and pizza, but Tasha, listen to this, Tasha just got offered a role in some TV sitcom. Can you believe it? She cheats on me, and she gets job offers." He swore again under his breath. "I'm sick of her. I'm sick of LA. I'm sick of the media."

Sam nodded. He could only imagine what his friend was going through. The salacious gossip was rife in Hollywood, yet another reason he didn't want to expose Paige to it.

Paige.

Her name.

God, he missed her so much.

"What's the matter with you? You got some dopey look on your face," Harry said. "Are you hung up on your *fake* girlfriend? The one you went to school with?"

Harry didn't need any more lies, so he answered truthfully. "Yep."

"Do you love her?"

"I don't know, I think so." He paused. "How do I know if it's love?"

"Don't ask me, I'm the worst person to ask about love," Harry said. "Speak to a shrink because if you ask me, I'll advise you to get a dog." His head fell back on the sofa, and he shut his eyes. "God, I wish I could erase seeing Tom and Tasha in bed." He rubbed his eyes as if to purge the memory.

"Why don't you find yourself a girlfriend? Not all women cheat," Sam said.

"I'm not interested in banging anyone…except Tasha's head between two cymbals." He sighed loudly. "It's been two weeks now and I still can't believe Tasha cheated on me."

"What's happening with your work transfer?"

"If I could just fly out of here and get a job in another country, I would. But it makes it easier with my visa to get a transfer." He cleared his throat. "It's either Melbourne or Hong Kong. I've already listed our house for sale."

"You're selling?"

"Yep. I moved out and have been living in a hotel for the past two weeks. I'm selling the house, giving Tasha half of everything and that's it." He sliced his hand through the air. "I'm not contesting or negotiating. Half/half. But if she starts with her demands, I'm gonna screw her over."

He was so angry and bitter. Sam clapped his hand on Harry's shoulder. "I'm sure her lawyer will do the right thing."

"She should've instructed her not to bang her husband's friends," Harry snapped. "Can I stay here tonight?"

"Sure, you know where the spare room is," Sam said, pointing to the doorway.

"Thanks Sam. And I'm sorry I have no advice about your girl, hope things work out." He stood and wobbled on his feet, before heading towards the hallway, which would take him to Sam's spare room. "G'night."

"Good night Harry," Sam called out, still on the sofa.

He checked his watch and easily calculated the time difference between LA and Melbourne. Perfect. He'd speak to his dad.

He'd avoided talking about anything personal and related to Paige, when he'd visited them, after returning from Queensland. They knew something was bothering him, and had subtly asked. But he just couldn't talk about it. Losing Paige was worse than all the movie rejections he'd received, bundled together, over his twenty-plus-year career.

His mum had hugged him, letting him know she was there when he was ready to talk.

Instead, they'd spent the day at home, his mum had made his favourite foods, and some close family members had dropped by. It had felt like Christmas and at the end of the day, he'd actually felt better having connected with his family.

Thinking back to that night after the snorkelling

and confessions on the boat was a stupid idea. It hurt. He clenched his fists, but the feelings of loss and rejections kept zipping along his veins.

The pain of pretending he was okay when he parted from her had been gut-wrenching. He'd hugged her hard, but because he had an image to maintain, even in front of his staff, he'd walked away.

Gah. Who was he? A star? A man? Both?

His defences crumbled as confusion and insecurity hitched in his chest. He swallowed hard. He should've spoken with his parents, but when he was with them a few days ago, he just couldn't. The words were stuck in his throat.

God, he was as pathetic as a teen moping.

He needed advice, and someone who'd be understanding. Lifting his cell, he dialled his father's number.

PAIGE WOKE on Saturday morning and stretched out her tired muscles. She hadn't slept well over the three weeks since she'd said goodbye to Sam.

Sam.

She missed him so much that it was like a physical ache in her heart.

She'd cried when she was alone. Tears of self-pity and also annoyance at herself for letting him go. But every time she reprimanded herself, she wondered how she'd manage living in LA under the media scrutiny. And, he'd never asked her.

She knew she was special to him. He'd said so in words and the way he'd made love to her. But she wasn't special enough for him to leave his career.

And then what?

Their time together had been in a bubble-like existence. Once reality set in, it would be very different. Just like Rachel had said.

She sighed. Her body was heavy, filled with feelings of defeat and self-blame. Could she have done more? She'd asked herself this question relentlessly for the past two weeks. The answer...she didn't know.

The weekend stretched out before her. Two full days and two full nights.

She didn't have any plans.

Perhaps she'd call Paisley and help her out, do some babysitting? That would kill a couple of hours. And then what. Watch more TV? Eat more ice-cream? Cry more tears?

Rachel and Travis were away for the weekend, so she couldn't even crash at her friend's place.

Hang out with her parents? They were social and were often busy each weekend.

Gosh, she felt like a total loser.

She stretched, stood and decided a run on the beach might help clear her mind. She'd have a look online and see if there were any cultural events or festivals on around the suburbs. It wasn't as much fun going alone as it was with a friend, but at least it was something to do.

Dressed in her running gear, she stretched her legs and arms, then jogged gently on the spot till she felt warm and her muscles ready for the ten-kilometre run.

Key? Check.

Music? Check.

All ready to go, when there was a knock at the door.

It was early, not that early. But too early for her neighbours to be up.

At the door, she looked through the peephole. *Sam?* "Sam, is that really you?"

"Yes. Do you want to open the door?"

She flung it open and just stared at him. "You're here." She rubbed her eyes, still quite unable to believe he was standing on her doorstep. Dressed in jeans that hugged his legs and butt all too well, he'd casually added a black T-shirt and black leather jacket over. His look was relaxed, yet sexy.

He smiled at her. "I've just come straight from the airport. Can I come inside?" He looked tired, but his eyes were dark and full of expectations. She took that as a good sign.

"Of course, sorry." She moved to the side and he strode in. A sense of deja-vu washed over her. Had it been a month ago that he'd stormed in here, accusing her of compromising him?

She closed the door and followed him in. "What's in there?" She pointed to the brown paper bag.

"Your favourite," he said with a grin.

Her eyelashes fluttered with surprise. "You've turned up on my doorstep and I don't know what to do."

"A kiss would be nice," he said placing the take-away coffee cups and brown paper bag on the side table.

"A kiss?" Her voice came across as squeaky as an old door that needed oiling. She was still in shock, seeing him. What was he doing here? The number of questions made her head hurt.

"We'll talk in a minute, but I just flew across the Pacific to be here so if you don't mind, I'd love a hug." He gave her a wink. "Come here," he said before pulling her into his arms.

CHAPTER 16

*H*e held her tight and just hugged her hard, loving the press of her body against his. For how many hours and days had he dreamt of this? He'd missed her so much that he'd been unable to focus on his work. Even his agent had snapped at him, reminding him he was a star and had responsibilities.

Yep, his agent was right, but his responsibilities extended to a tall woman who was smart, funny and made him happy.

And now she was in his arms, where she belonged. Her arms were around his waist, and his head rested on top of hers. The scent of her filled his nose, and a calmness settled upon him. In her exercise gear, he'd been able to admire her toned body and long legs.

She stepped back and her face showed that she was still quite unable to believe he was in her apartment. He brushed the worry lines from her forehead. "Paige darling, everything is fine. I needed to talk to you...and no, I didn't want to use the phone."

He handed her a coffee cup. "A latte, just the way you like it, and your favourite almond croissant."

"Thank you," she took the cup and sat on the sofa, and waved her arms for him to join her.

He grabbed his coffee and sat opposite her. He'd practised what he was going to say on the long plane ride over but now, with her sitting there, he forgot everything he wanted to say. The eloquent lines he'd prepared were gone and his mouth dried, with nerves.

"I've missed you," he said. *Brilliant. How pathetic was that?* He missed her. Gah. He reprimanded himself. He was an actor and used to learning his lines, yet his mind was blank.

"I've missed you too," she said. "But you didn't need to fly here to tell me that."

Her eyes were filled with questions and warmth, so he took that as a positive sign. Taking a deep breath, he reached down to his core where he had been hurting for so long and exposed himself for the first time.

"I'm an actor and am surrounded by people who

say yes to me. They tell me what I want to hear." He paused. "But you, like my parents, I trust. We have history, but I know that you won't tell me what I want to hear. You'll always tell me the truth. And that's very different for me. For years, all I've heard is how good I am. And it's usually because they want something from me."

She nodded but didn't say anything. Coffee forgotten, her focus was on him.

"I built a wall around me, like a self-defence mechanism. No one could get through, that way, I never got hurt. The only people I trust are my staff, like Megan, my agent and my lawyer."

"What about friends?"

"The only real friend I have is Harry." He blew out a long breath of frustration. "I go to parties and events, and I'm surrounded by people who like me, but I don't have any *real* friends." He ran his fingers through his hair. "My trip to Australia changed me. Seeing you again reminded me of the school friends I'd left behind. I'd kept in touch with *no one*. And then the date. Oliver. What a nice guy. In that short time we spent together, I was reminded of what it was like having friends and having fun."

"You're one of Hollywood's leading actors."

"That's right. I've been working since I was five, and in Hollywood for twelve years and I never realised how tired I was till I met up with you. It's like in the Wizard of Oz movie where everything is in colour and no longer black and white. I'm seeing everything differently." It was the best way that he could explain his feelings. The time in Australia had changed him in such a way that he couldn't go back to how things had been.

He sipped his coffee, to moisten his mouth, before placing it back on the table. "I've never questioned my career choice or my lifestyle, but coming here has made me do that. I, um, I want more than to be just an actor. I want friends, and I want to do the stuff we used to do like go on picnics, go to the beach, kick a footy in the park."

A frown marred her forehead, and he could see that something was niggling her.

"This is a revelation. I would never have expected this from you. I mean, you are a star. You have the world at your feet, so to speak." She leaned over and sipped her coffee. "I'm glad you've made this decision, but I'm not sure why you felt the need to fly all the way here. It's a fourteen-hour plane ride."

He'd botched things up. He was floundering. Bugger. He placed her cup on the coffee table, and took her hands in his. "What I'm trying to say is that I want it all, but I want it with you."

Her mouth opened into an O, and her eyes widened with shock.

"I want to find a way that I can be a husband, a father, a son and a friend, without damaging the people I love around me." He took a steadying breath. "I've got ideas, but I want us to work on this *together*."

She shook her head and then stood. Hands on her hips, she glared at him. "You told me you didn't love me, and you left me. I understand you're lonely and missing Harry, but that doesn't mean I'm here for you as a second-place prize."

"No," he said. "That's not what I meant."

Her face softened. "I'm not following, so maybe try again."

He gestured for her to sit next to him. "Megan rearranged my calendar so I could fly here to see you, I have to fly back tonight."

"You're here only for the day?" Her voice was filled with astonishment.

"Yep. I had to see you, work things out." He caressed the pulse point on her wrist. "You are the best thing that has happened to me. I trust you. I want to be with you. And I love you."

He heard her gasp but he continued. "It took me too long to realise it, but I do love you. You're the one I want to be with…always. I want to create a life with you, and when we're ready, we'll have a family." He paused. "Both our parents have been happily married, and I want that with you. We have issues to work through, but I know that you are the one I want to wake up to every morning. The one I want to eat fish and chips with, go to the beach with, and watch TV with. You make me so happy, and I can't imagine not having you in my life, not just as a friend but as a life partner."

"I want that, too, but I don't know if I can. The pressures of who you are, are massive, and it's going to impact us." She rubbed her eyes. "I'm clumsy, I'm not polished, I'm just…just me."

"And that's what I love about you, you're amazing. You're real, you're beautiful, and you're fun to be with." He sliced his hand through the air. "I don't care about parties and events. I'd much rather be with you."

"But for how long? Is this really what you want. You can't just step down. The media will hound us, and you'll be dealing with the fall-out. It will be my fault. I don't want to do that to you."

"Paige, darling, we're going to work it out… together." He sat straighter, excited to share his plans with her. "Tell me if you like this. I have a movie to do, I'm contracted, but we're going to organise for you to come and be on set with me. After that, I'm scaling back my work." He paused. "I'm going to sell my house in the hills and we're going to move to a small town. There are heaps of beautiful towns in California. We'll find one together. We'll have a home there, and I will commute to LA when I work. I'm not going to work the way I have been. I will be more selective on what shows and movies I do. And until we have children, you will be with me." His heart thudded in anticipation of the new life they would create, and he hoped she would love it as much as he did. He was scaling back his work for her. He was giving up potential blockbusters for her. He was reorganising his life for her.

"I have to give up my life here, then?" She gave him a despondent frown.

He replied with an exasperated sigh. "Yes, sort of." They both had to give and take, to close the distances between them. "You'll be starting a new life with me in California. We'll have a large home so your family can visit and stay with us. We'll make friends together. We'll be a couple and then a family, but we'll do it together. I can see this working for us." He was so sure that she would be delighted to hear his proposal that he hadn't considered, not once on the flight over, that she wouldn't be interested.

"But what about my job, my career."

He could hear the upset in her voice. "I know. You'd have to give up your career here." He confirmed. "But we could look at you becoming qualified in America, and you could be an engineer there. Or you could follow your mum's footsteps and start your own kitchen, helping those in need, or you could help me with my charity projects. Or you could start your own, helping smart students who come from disadvantaged backgrounds achieve. You could mentor them, help them with maths and science. There are some great kids, who through no fault of their own, have crappy home lives. You could help them. You're so smart. They'd be so lucky to have you mentor them." The words tumbled from his lips. There were so many opportunities for her. He knew she loved her job, but he'd help her find something just as good in America. Melbourne was not the only place for jobs.

Paige fell back on the sofa and rubbed her eyes. "I don't know."

The breath left him, and he felt his face fall. He'd stuffed up. The issues were too great between them. Despite all the suggestions and his declaration of love, her career and the media issue was going to keep them apart. He wasn't sure if she was considering his alternatives or just using the issues to keep them apart.

Massaging the pain away in his heart, he said, "I do love you. I flew here to find a way that we could overcome the barriers between us. I thought you would like what I was suggesting." He paused. "You don't. And it seems that I'm asking too much of you. I'm sorry. Guess I'm not the guy for you." He leaned over and brushed his lips against hers. "I've got a few hours left before my return flight so I'm going to visit Mum and Dad. Bye." What was the use in staying? Not once during his impassioned speech had she agreed with him. No nod. No ah-ha. No "that's a great idea."

She hadn't liked his compromises.

Sighing with disappointment, his shoulders slumped with defeat. At least he'd tried.

He'd missed an important meeting in LA to be here now, and it had been worth it, even if Paige had rejected him.

He'd gone after his girl, been honest, and tried to win her back.

Shame he hadn't been successful.

Being hounded by the media was not fun. He was tired of not being able to go out in public without being photographed or approached by fans.

He enjoyed meeting his fans, but there were

times he just wanted to be left alone. But that wasn't going to happen.

He'd forgotten who he was. And he'd remembered and found that person in Australia with Paige. And then, to a smaller extent with Oliver.

Having friends and reconnecting with those he loved was how he wanted to spend his life. But there would always be the press. He understood her concerns. It wasn't easy living his life.

"Goodbye, Paige." He stood and walked to the front door. Turning, he saw that she was still slumped on the sofa, her eyes closed and her face marred with indecision.

Rejected.

He waited thirty seconds but she didn't call out to him.

Dammit.

The life he'd imagined with her faded, and he closed the door behind him. He signalled to his driver, who patiently sat waiting for him.

Turning one last time, he saw that the front door to her apartment remained shut.

He sighed, as despondency made his face fall. It was over.

He and his ideas had been well and truly rejected.

"I'm visiting my parents, let's go," he said to the driver.

* * *

PAIGE SAT ON THE SOFA, her head filled with questions and disbelief. Could she simply just leave everyone and live in a small town in California? She'd only be able to see her nephew grow through video conferencing. Would he forget her?

And her parents? She'd see them once a year. Could she do that? And Rachel? No more chats, walks, movie nights and fun with her. She'd have to find new friends.

She felt deflated and worn out.

Sam had confessed his love to her, something she'd always wanted and dreamt of... but it came with conditions. She wasn't sure that she could work with those conditions. Would she still be *her*? Or would she just be known as Sam's partner?

And there was still the issue of the media pressure. Moving to a small town wouldn't help. There would always be the problem of them being stalked or photographed.

What a mess.

Leaning over, she drained the last of her coffee. She looked around and realised he'd left. Her thoughts had consumed her so much that she hadn't noticed him leaving.

How had that happened? How had he left and she not noticed?

Her stomach hardened with disbelief.

What to do? What to do?

She wanted to be with Sam...but at what cost to her? Could she give up her life here, for him? She couldn't expect him to move here, there wasn't enough work in Australia.

He had made concessions and compromises. And had she listened? No, not really. Her focus had been on her job. Her job that she'd almost lost after her time away with Sam.

Her manager had been furious that she'd taken so much leave without consideration for her team or the project she was working on. She'd been reprimanded.

She had her job, she had her family, she had her friends. But was she truly happy? Before she met Sam again, she would've said yes. Now there was a piece of her missing. Could they work things out? Was it possible? Her heart skittered with excitement.

He'd flown here to see her. And she'd virtually ignored him. It wasn't rudeness that made her do it, but rather shock and excitement at seeing him this morning. The surprise of him visiting had shaken her to her core.

Since they'd said goodbye after the snorkelling

outing, she never expected to see him again, except on screen or in social media.

But he'd come after her. And she was going to do the same with him. Grabbing her purse and keys, she headed outside so she could drive to his parents' house. She just hoped they still lived in the same house they had all those years ago.

CHAPTER 17

*P*aige knocked on the door of the modest, brick home in one of Melbourne's leafy suburbs. The retro house, built in the 1950s, was the same but it looked better than she remembered, with the freshly painted wooden trellises, rose garden and overall prettiness.

Did Sam's parents still live here? She gulped at her nerves. She hoped so.

The door opened and it was Sam.

The relief of seeing him, and knowing she was at the correct address made her sag against the wall.

"Paige? Are you okay?" A look of concern crossed his face, and he took a step towards her, taking her forearm.

"Yeah, just nervous. I wasn't sure if this was the right house, and if you would be here," she confessed, feeling as nervous as a teen on her first serious date.

"Come in, Mum's made breakfast," he said, tugging her towards him.

"Um." She looked around, wondering if she was intruding on private family time.

"Do you mind making a decision inside, I don't want the neighbours to see me here?"

"Of course." He was a star, the media would "hound" his parents if they knew he was here in Australia. "Sorry."

She stepped into the house and was greeted by the comforting smells of toast and coffee.

Closing the door behind her, he leaned against it, his arms across his chest. "What do you want?"

"I want to talk with you," she said. "I handled this morning really badly and I came to apologise."

"You could've called, but, um, I'm glad you're here." He gestured to the back of the house. "Just come and say hi first, they'd love to see you."

"Okay," she said, following him down the hall. She took a moment to look around. The house was familiar but looked so much better than she remembered with its beautiful furnishings. It had an eclectic mix of modern and retro pieces that blended well, and the modest house had a comforting feel about it.

Photos of Sam dotted the walls, artfully arranged, all showcasing his incredible contribution to the arts community in Australia and America. There were also family portraits included, and she could see that Sam had inherited his dark eyes and dark hair from his father.

"Mum, Dad," he called out. "Paige has dropped in."

After a flurry of hugs, greetings, and inquiries about her family, Sam excused them. "Let me talk to Paige, and then we'll join you for breakfast."

She caught a look between his parents before they nodded in agreement.

"Let's go outside, we'll have privacy there, I'll just get my jacket."

Minutes later, they sat on the patio, on an outdoor lounge setting. The morning winter air was cold, and Sam turned on an outdoor heater which provided some warmth.

"I haven't really worked out what I was going to say," she said, as they sat across from each other. Her heart started to pound against her chest, and her nerves made her fingers tremble. "I-um, I didn't expect to see you again, except at the movies, of course, and seeing you this morning has um, I mean, I just didn't expect it. It was a shock."

"It's okay," he reassured her. She could see his dark eyes were filled with concern and interest.

"It's not okay. I was rude to you this morning because I was stunned. I don't recall when you left. I'm sorry." She pressed her lips together and hoped she could get her words out. She sat on her hands so he wouldn't see how nervous she was.

"You offered me an amazing suggestion, an opportunity for us to be together. And I do like it. And I want to say yes, but I need to ask you. Will you be happy? I mean, you're giving up so much. Will I make you happy? And will *you* be happy?"

He smiled and his face lit up. "I see pictures of myself everywhere. And I can't go out anywhere. I don't trust anyone, I don't have friends. I didn't realise what I wanted till we reconnected."

Her heart leapt with surprise. "Really?"

"Really. It wasn't till we were together, and the date with Oliver, that I realised what I was missing. You. Family. Friends."

His confession made her jaw drop and her eyes widen. "I can't believe it's what you want. I mean, you are a star and—"

"Yeah, I am. But I'm a man first, and if I have to choose between a life and a career, I've chosen life." He stopped and smiled at her. "I love acting, but I'm lonely. I'm surrounded by people but have no true friends except for Harry. I never let anyone close to me. But with you, I can. I trust you. You know me too well. And I love that you are you. I love that you are smart and sensible. You're beautiful, caring, and devoted to your family."

She stifled a sob, unable to believe what she was hearing.

"I'm happy when I'm with you, truly happy. Something I rarely feel," he confessed.

"I'll still work but I can choose what I do, and it will leave me time to work on my charity projects. I want to do things *with you*, help others *with you*, be *with you*."

"You won't get bored, or frustrated that you're not going to be in the limelight anymore?" She was still worried that he'd find their new life boring.

"Are you kidding me? I can't wait to have a more normal life. You and me. It's going to take time for you to settle in, but after the movie, we'll visit some towns in California and then buy a place that we both love. We'll have privacy and live a quiet life. And I'll do some movies or TV work, and I'll commute."

"Are you sure?"

"Tell me you love me?" He smiled, and his eyes blazed with longing.

"I love you," she said with meaning.

He stood and walked to her. "I love you, and we're going to make this work."

Helping her to a standing position, he took both her hands in his. "Megan and my team will help you. If you need an outfit, they'll make sure you look fabulous. I want you to be happy. I will make sure that you can manage the media but eventually, they'll tire of me and you."

"We'll be too boring for them," she said with anticipation.

"Exactly," he said with a grin. "There are plenty of actors and enough gossip in LA, that the media will eventually lose interest. When I do a movie, you'll be with me. You'll have stylists on hand to help."

"Awhile back, you asked me what I would do if I could do anything?"

He nodded in reply. "I remember, you said you weren't sure."

"Yes. But what I didn't tell you was that I did want to find love. Love with someone who had the same values as me. You and I are like that. We give back to society, we love our families, and we work in jobs we like." Her breathing came in rapid bursts as she continued with her confession. "I love being an engineer but I also love working with disadvantaged women, and also washing dogs with children. I don't have a dream job but there are so many things that I like to do, that I know that I'll find a purpose in America. . .with you."

His mouth opened, and she pressed a finger against his lips.

"Let me finish, please," she asked. "I'll need you to help me find my *purpose* whether I mentor, support your charity or go through the process so that I can work as an engineer in America. I just need you to help me."

"Always. I want you to be happy. And, we can come home, to Australia and visit our families, or we fly them to California."

His sincerity calmed her rapidly beating heart.

"There are a lot of companies in America that would love to have you work for them. We'll find you a job you love, whether it's as an engineer or scientist."

Trepidation made her chest tighten but she needed to be upfront for them to be successful together. "I need to ask something else of you?"

He nodded. "Of course."

"I need help with the media. I'll need you to give me a hug and reassure me when things are hard." She took a steadying breath. "And I need you to protect me. You understand Hollywood, I don't."

"Always. I know this industry. Trust me on keeping you safe." He paused. "And I agree to everything else. I want you to be happy. Whatever you want, I will be there for you."

She felt her eyes fill with warm tears of gratitude.

"I want to kiss you so badly," he said in a low voice.

"And I want you to kiss me so badly," she said with a lift of her eyebrow.

His mouth crashed on hers as his arms came around her waist. He kissed her as though he were starving for her. They kissed and kissed.

He tugged her close, and held her against him. "There will be times when it will be hard, but we'll deal with it together. I want you in my life, always and forever." He stepped away and lifted her hands, so he could kiss her knuckles. "I love you so much that I am bursting with love. If things get too hard, you need to promise me that you'll tell me."

"I promise," she said.

"I think I forgot something," a funny look crossed his eyes.

"What?" she asked curious as to what was missing.

"I forgot to ask you to marry me," he said.

She gasped. "Oh wow."

"But, I'm not going to. I'd like to do this properly. Let's go and tell my parents our good news, then we'll visit your parents, and I can speak to them."

"You're going to ask my parents about marrying me?" Her eyes narrowed in surprise.

"I'm taking you away from them. I think it's only fair that I reassure them of my love for you, and how I will look after and care for you. Besides, I want them to know they are welcome to visit anytime."

"Anytime?" she asked in an exaggerated voice.

"Almost anytime." He brushed his lips against hers. "Come on, let's tell our parents the good news."

Hand in hand, they walked to the door that would lead them to his parents, and she was bursting with excitement.

She trusted Sam, and knew that he would do everything right for her.

They'd have their ups and downs, like all couples did. But with Sam, she'd found the guy she wanted to spend the rest of her life with, and raise a family with. Everything else, would be worked out... together. She didn't think she'd be able to wipe the grin from her lips. Everything was going to be perfect.

*P*hoebe stood next to her two sisters under a canopy of white flowers; her older sister Paige was about to marry her high school crush, Sam Balfer.

He stood patiently next to his best friend Harry. They were whispering to themselves and giving each other friendly looks, that only good mates do.

There were moments when she wanted to pinch herself, quite unable to believe her sister, Paige, was marrying a Hollywood star. Her gaze took in the beautiful outdoor wedding that Paige had organised. Amazing. Her klutzy, vibrant, geeky sister had found this hidden gem in the Dandenongs and their wedding was nothing short of spectacular.

Phoebe was bursting with pride at how well all the details from the artfully arranged flowers, to the scented candles and twinkle lights, had been organised. The effect was romantic and oh-so-pretty. Very unusual for her sister, who favoured jeans and T-shirts, and skated on a skateboard. It seemed love does make you go crazy, because she would never have expected such a beautiful setting for her tomboy sister.

The reception centre, accessed via a private road, was hidden amongst beautiful natural forest. With the security firm protecting the property's perimeter, Sam and Paige were able to enjoy their small wedding amongst family and friends. The weather in February was warm, and the ceremony was being held outdoors, no need for the back-up chapel.

Phoebe, like her sisters, was dressed in navy blue, each wearing a dress that suited their figures, unlike Poppy who was wearing pants.

She'd chosen to wear a designer dress, with a plunging front and back which showcased her model body to perfection. It was so figure-hugging that she hadn't been able to wear underwear, but she didn't care. She felt fabulous, and as a model, it made sense for her to look sensational. Besides, her body was her business card, and she always looked her best.

The harpist started to gracefully pluck the strings with her long fingers, and all heads turned to the back. In walked her little nephew, Lev, wearing a suit and holding a basket of petals. The last time she'd seen him, he was a baby and now he was a toddler.

Living in London for the past few years had meant that she'd missed time with her family and seeing Lev grow. A tinge of pain flickered in her chest, but she dismissed it.

Her career was overseas, not here. And soon, she was going to be famous. Having been selected to work on Serena Millinova, yes, Serena Millinova's Cinderella Project with Oliver Baden, model extra-ordinaire, she knew that her modelling career was going to skyrocket and she was going to be famous. This was the break she'd been working towards for the past five years. *Finally*.

Returning her attention to the wedding, she watched her nephew sprint down the aisle on his little legs. "Mum-mmmm-eeee," he squealed, before heading towards her sister Paisley.

"Did I do good?" he asked, loud enough that everyone heard.

"Yes, my angel," Paisley reassured him in a soft voice.

Phoebe resisted the urge to roll her eyes at Pais-ley's lie. Lev hadn't done well, he was supposed to scatter rose petals on the carpet before Paige walked down; and he was still holding the basket full of petals.

Her gaze took in Paisley smiling at her son, her face filled with love for him. Paisley never complained about being a single mum. Nope, she'd taken it all in her stride.

Phoebe had begged her sister to tell her ex about Lev, but Paisley wouldn't, insisting she knew what was best for them both.

Paisley was her twin, and she'd reluctantly agreed to say nothing.

They were so different. They looked similar, but Paisley was quiet, maternal, and a home-body. Paisley's idea of a good night in was watching some Disney movie with her son. Urgh. Boring.

Whereas she loved to flaunt her body in skin-tight dresses and stilettos, dance the night away, and drink way too many cocktails.

She wasn't interested in getting married or having children. Maybe one day, but not now. She loved the parties she attended. Her career was important to her and she intended on being world-famous.

The music changed with the arrival of the bride, interrupting Phoebe's focus on herself. Looking up, Paige walked in, flanked by her parents.

Had Paige worn denim jeans, Phoebe wouldn't have been surprised. But she hadn't.

Paige had found a simple off-white, lace dress that clung to her slim curves and suited her height. Flowers decorated the simple up-do of her hair, and she carried a simple posy of white flowers.

Phoebe smiled. Paige looked stunning, and her smile was so wide that there was no doubt that she was so happy to be marrying Sam.

Even her mum and dad were beaming with joy and pride.

And as she always did, Phoebe stole a look at the groom. Sam's smile matched Paige's.

He stepped forward to meet Paige and her parents. He gave his future mother-in-law a kiss on the cheek before shaking her dad's hand. Sam promised both of them that he would love and care for their daughter.

Walking hand in hand to the canopy, Sam and Paige stood in front of the clergyman who performed the ceremony.

Tears stung her eyes as Sam and Paige each promised to love each other in front of family and friends. And she saw that Sam's mum and her mum were also a little teary-eyed.

Only the best man, Harry, stood taken aback.

There was no smile, and he looked sad and forlorn, a real contrast to everyone else.

And then it was over. Sam and Paige were married, and everyone clapped as they had their first kiss as a married couple.

The parents from both families hugged and kissed, and then the sisters enveloped their parents in a group hug.

The happy couple and their parents greeted and kissed guests, whilst the three unmarried sisters hung back.

"I'm so happy that Paige is married," Paisley cooed, still cradling Lev.

"Well it's unlikely that either of us are going to get hitched," Phoebe replied with a pfft.

The beaming smile slipped from Paisley's face, and Phoebe's heart skipped a beat for upsetting her twin. "I'm sorry."

Paisley shook her head. "It's okay." She kissed her son, before lowering him to the ground. Still holding Lev's hand, she said, "Phoebs, you're an international model and Poppy's a bit kooky." She turned her gaze to her sister, standing to her right, and then pointed out her shoes which were black and white, like a Dalmatian dog print. "I mean, it'd take someone pretty special to put up with you and your obsession with dogs."

Her older sister, Poppy, bumped her with her shoulder. "Liking dogs isn't kooky. Anyway, *love me, love my dogs* is my motto."

Her sisters chuckled in reply.

"And that's why you're going to be a spinster, surrounded by dogs," Phoebe added before lifting her perfectly groomed eyebrow, giving her an *I know more than you* look.

"Could be worse. I could be a spinster and no dogs," Poppy clarified with a waggle of her eyebrows.

Paisley chuckled. "You never know. Maybe you and Harry will get together." She nudged Phoebe and her gaze settled on the handsome man who was Sam's best man.

Poppy sighed dramatically. "I don't think so. He seems quite revolted by the whole marriage thing." She paused and looked at her younger sister. "You're an international model, and I'm busy with my dog business."

Poppy glanced down at her nephew who didn't seem to be interested in what his mum and aunties were discussing. Looking at Paisley she said, "What about you? Do you think…"

"No," Paisley said, with a soulful look in her eyes. "He made a decision, and he's working in America." She pressed her lips together as though needing a moment to compose herself. "Do you honestly think *he'd* come back and settle down? Be a husband and a father?"

Phoebe's heart ached for her twin. Paisley deserved to be happy, and she deserved a man to be with. And her nephew deserved a dad.

As though reading her thoughts, her twin's eyes darkened and she shook her head. "Don't say it." Paisley snapped at her. "He's famous now. I don't want my son being exposed to his lifestyle. You really think being on the road, with drugs, drinking, and groupies is a good lifestyle for my son, your nephew?"

Phoebe's throat tightened with hurt for her sister, who'd been left pregnant and alone by the love of her life. The man who'd used and betrayed her.

"I'm a single mum. I'm working and have a child to care for. Just let it go, will you?" Paisley's plea was filled with so much emotional angst that Phoebe's heart ached in pain.

There were times Phoebe wanted to betray her twin and tell her now-famous ex about his son. But Paisley would kill her. And her loyalty lay with her twin, not some loser rocker. "Sure, I just want you to be happy."

"I am." Paisley gave her a watery smile. "Come on, Paige has just married Sam. Can you believe it? Sam

Balfer," she said in a bright voice. "Sam's my brother-in-law, how cool is that?"

"Very cool," Phoebe agreed. "When you rang to tell me about Paige and Sam, I never expected them to marry, but they're cute together. They're meant to be."

Paisley smiled at her. "Yep, they are."

"Come on, let's give Mum and Dad a hug. Come on Poppy." She tugged her sisters towards her, and then they spent time hugging their parents and Sam's parents.

A FEW HOURS later after the official photos, everyone was relaxed at the reception, and Harry stood and walked to the microphone. As the best man, he was obliged to make a speech and it was the last thing he wanted to do. Today had been a type of torture. All he could think about was how badly his marriage had ended. Only a few years ago, he'd married Tasha who he thought was the love of his life and the woman he wanted to grow old with. But she'd betrayed him in the worst way. Not just having an affair but fucking his friend.

The image of his friend's head buried between Tasha's legs still haunted him at night, when he often couldn't sleep. Darn them. As a way of dealing with his anger, he'd taken up boxing. Every time he punched, he thought about his ex-friend, Tom. And when he trained with the bag, he'd stuck a photo of Tom there. Punch, punch, punch. Take that, loser.

Not only had he lost his wife, but also his friend.

He hated them both.

At least he was away from LA, and now living in Hong Kong.

The Asian city was so different from living in the Hollywood hills, which allowed him to finally exorcise the pain of his marriage breakdown.

And last week, he'd even gone on a date.

And enjoyed it.

From the typed sheet, he read his short speech in a clear voice. There was nothing in his tone to betray him of the angst bottled inside. Nope, only he knew of that.

After complimenting each of the bridesmaids, Paige's sisters, his gaze met Poppy's. She smiled back and his chest tightened, which surprised him. He took a deep breath before he wished Sam and Paige all the best.

Lies tumbled from his lips as he talked about enduring love and how special marriage was.

Everyone nodded and smiled.

But marriage was like that. It sucked...and so did having your wife bang your best friend.

Marriage suited Sam and Paige. They were deliriously happy and in love, just like he'd been once upon a time.

Lifting a glass of sparkling wine, he toasted the happy couple, who then kissed.

He was happy for Sam but he just couldn't allow himself to let go of his pain. Could he ever trust again? Maybe. Marry again? No way.

For now, his focus was his job, and that was it.

He'd return to Hong Kong tomorrow, to his predictable life, and that suited him fine.

After finishing his speech, Sam and Paige cut the cake, more photos were taken and then the couple danced together.

Sam had only one best man, him, there were no other groomsmen. Whereas Paige had three sisters and her best friend, Rachel, as bridesmaids.

Rachel danced with her fiancé.

Paisley danced with her son.

Phoebe danced with a cousin.

Poppy danced with him.

Dancing with Poppy suited him. She was nice, interesting and seemed genuinely kind.

He walked over, held out his hand and accompanied her to the dance floor.

"That was a very nice speech you made," she said with a sweet smile.

He liked that she fit perfectly in his arms as they swayed to the music. "Thank you."

"I'm a terrible dancer. I'm sorry that you got stuck with me," she said with a wink.

He didn't mind. He'd been actually happy to be allocated to dance with Poppy. He'd been relieved that Phoebe had been partnered with a cousin, who had flown in from overseas. Phoebe was sex on legs, and she was just *too much* for him.

Too many times he'd had to compose himself. The pain of losing what he had was torturing him over this weekend.

Taking a steady breath, he gazed at his dancing partner. Out of the three single sisters, he liked Poppy the best with her quirky humour and love of dogs.

They swayed together, and he could smell the citrusy scent of her, shampoo? Body wash? He wasn't sure. He lifted his arm so she could twirl clockwise, and then he twirled her again, the other way.

Back in his arms she smiled at him. "You're a good dancer, I've enjoyed spending time with you over the past couple of days."

He nodded. He'd enjoyed talking to her. In fact,

there was so much that he liked about Poppy that he was a little disappointed that he was leaving tomorrow.

"You look lovely, by the way," he said, admiring the jumpsuit she wore.

The elegant outfit showcased her slim body and the off-the-shoulder top hinted at sexy rather than announced it on a mega-phone, like her younger sister had.

"Thanks. I'm not really into dresses, and when I saw this outfit, I just knew it would be perfect. I was so happy that Paige didn't mind me wearing pants instead of a dress," she confessed in a low voice.

He nodded. She looked sensational in her outfit, and he had been impressed by her confidence to wear something that wasn't very bridesmaidy.

"Considering this is the first time I've seen Paige wear a dress, I think that's only fair," he added with a chuckle.

She gave him a grin that made his tummy tumble. When she smiled, her whole face lit up, and she was so pretty.

His chest lifted and he realised that he was feeling a lot happier than he had for a long time. They continued to dance, surrounded by couples.

Feeling her pressed up against him was a type of

torture. For the first time in a long time, his body was responding to a woman.

This hadn't happened in a very long time.

But she was all wrong for him, and she was the bride's sister.

Wong, wrong, wrong.

Nope, he wasn't going to do anything about it, even if he did have the uncanny urge to lean down and brush his lips against hers.

He resisted. It was better this way.

He had no intention of any long-term or lasting relationships for now. And Poppy deserved better than a one-night stand, because that was all he had to give.

No. He liked and respected her too much. Better to be social media friends, than anything else.

Besides, he was returning to Hong Kong the following day. So for the night, he'd dance, he'd have some fun, he'd enjoy time with Poppy.

Tomorrow he was leaving Melbourne, and wouldn't be returning.

His career was important to him, and that was based in Asia.

Poppy deserved better than him. Definitely.

ACKNOWLEDGMENTS

Dear Reader

One of the perks of being a romance author is that I can admit to looking at pics of good-looking guys and claim that it's all part of my job—LOL.

For those who follow me on social media, you will know that I have a tiny. . .okay, a more than tiny, fan-girl crush on the Scottish actor Sam Heughan, who seems to be as charming in real life as he is on screen.

When I was creating my characters for *Want You*, I saw Sam's video about going on a date with him. And it was then that I knew I'd found my hero for this book.

Handsome, talented, and the superstar women dream of meeting. So, who better to pair him with than his teenage friend? Paige is the eldest but the quietist of four sisters. She's the smart one who lives in the shadows of her sisters.

I really loved writing this book, and I hope you love reading it.

This is the first book of the Finding Love series, and although all the books have connecting characters, each book is a standalone and can be read without having read others.

I hope you love this series as much as I'm loving all the characters and creating a rocky but fun road for each of them to find love.

Thank you to my amazing family and friends who are so supportive of my writing. I am grateful to have them in my life cheering and encouraging me to be an author.

And to my professional cheer squad, thank you to the team who make my books shine. My amazing editor, Jena O'Connor, my wonderful proofreader, Janice Owen, and my talented artist Erin Cawood.

This book is for all the geeky girls out there who thought the cute guy would never notice them. Well…he did.

Happy reading, Joanne xo

FINDING LOVE

 ear Reader

I HOPE you enjoyed reading **Want You**. All the books in the Finding Love series are standalone reads but have interconnecting characters.

WANT to know what happens to Phoebe when she returns to London for the job of a lifetime? If you love marriage of convenience romances, and romantic comedies then you'll love **Marry Me.**

.   .   .

WANT to know what happens to Poppy? Do she and Harry stand a chance when he's broken and she's not interested in a relationship? If you love dogs and friends-to-lovers romances, then you'll love *Meet You.*

WHY WAS PAISLEY A SINGLE MUM? Will Lev get to meet his dad? If you love rockstars, and secret-baby romances, then you'll love *Need You.*

AND WHAT ABOUT RACHEL? She thinks she and Travis have a solid relationship. Perhaps not. Find out what happens to her in *Ask You.*

SAM AND PAIGE may have their happily-ever-after, but what about the hard-working Megan? She's not going to be happy babysitting Paige and losing status as Sam's right-hand woman in Hollywood. Want to read her HEA? Then check out *Find You.*

CHECK out my website for all the news and updates of this fab series, and also my other books.

WITH LOVE, Joanne x

*D*id you know that I write both sweet, and sexy books?

SWEET – my sweet reads are generally my holiday romances which focuses on the emotional journey of the hero and heroine. There are usually no bedroom scenes but if there is, it is closed doors (you, as the reader do not "see" these scenes)

Sexy – my sexy reads have a heat level of 3 out of 5. There will be a couple of love making scenes, the bedroom door is open (meaning, you read the scene) but the journey of the hero and heroine is emotional not sexual.

. . .

ON MY WEBSITE, I've noted the heat level against each of my books to help you know if the read is sweet or sexy.

SIGN up to my newsletter where I share news on my latest books, insights in to my writing and recommend romances I've read; and to say thanks I'll send you a free e-copy of **Bidding on Love**.

https://joannedannon.com/free-offer-for-bidding-on-love/

THE KISSING DOWN UNDER SERIES

*B*ook 1 **Kissing under the Spotlight**
- Can a superstar singer croon his way into the heart of an ordinary girl?

Book 2 Kissing like she means it
- The plan was not to fall in love. Can friends with benefits have a happily ever after?

Book 3 Kissing her brother's best friend
- Should she lie to her brother and kiss his best friend?

Book 4 Kissing him at last
- It's never a good idea to fall for your best friend's brother... or so they say.

The Kissing Down Under series has been designed

333

so you don't have to read them in order. They are each standalone romances with no cliff hangers.

However, you will most likely enjoy reading them in order.

Happy reading, Joanne x

HOLIDAY ROMANCES

*I*f you love the Hallmark channel, and books focussing on love, family, community, with a splash of faith, then these sets are for you -

DREAMING of Christmas

DREAMING of Hanukah

Christmas Kiss series

*I*f you love romances with characters that are flawed or broken, dealing with issues such as fidelity, and drug/alcohol abuse, then these romances are for you.

Note. These books have swear words, unlike my other romances.

FALLING for the Best Man

Not your average romance. *When the love of his life is his brother's bride-to-be...*

When he's asked to be the best man at their wedding, should he speak up, or forever hold his peace?

. . .

FALLING for Miss Write

A complex romance where both the hero and heroine are struggling to overcome their past mistakes.

BOXED SET ROMANCES

*L*ove to read? Need more romances? Then check out these boxed sets with hours of blissful reading.

DREAMING Of Christmas
    Dreaming of Hanukah
    Kissing Down Under
    New York Romance
    Another Unforgettable Holiday